BONE & LORAINE

by

KEN FARMER

Cover by: K.R. Farmer
Art Work: Adriana Girolami
Cover Model - Vivian Jimenez Hall

FOREWARD
by
Marshall R. Teague - Veteran Actor, Ret. Navy, former Deputy Sheriff

When I was a child. I dreamed of being a Cowboy in the old West. I read every book and watched every TV show that had my Western Hero's atop their mighty steeds, all of which had Great names like Champion, Trigger, Dollor, Topper, Tony, and Black Jack.

Today, having done Eighteen Western Films and Television shows, many of which were taken right out of the pages of Western writers of high acclaim. Writers like Louis L'Amour, Terry C. Johnston, Zane Gray and Ken Farmer, who have kept the Western lore very much alive now and for Generations to come.

Novelist, Ken Farmer, whose books I have become obsessed with, captures every element which draws the reader back in time and places them at the same camp fire alongside the many colorful characters that you feel you have always known. Names like Flynn, Fiona, Bass, Bone, Loraine and Lucy, just to name a few you will become very familiar with.

Don't be surprised if, along the way, you pick up a touch of Shakespeare, History…past and present, along with what one might say…A Look at Our Future…Saddle Up, You're in for *A Hell of a Ride*!

Marshall & Lindy Teague

ISBN-13: - 978-1-7329119-2-5
ISBN-10: - 1-7329119-2-4
Timber Creek Press
Imprint of Timber Creek Productions, LLC
312 N. Commerce St.
Gainesville, Texas 76240

Published by: Timber Creek Press
timbercreekpresss@yahoo.com
www.timbercreekpress.net
Twitter: @pagact
Facebook Book Page:
www.facebook.com/TimberCreekPress
Ken's email: pagact@yahoo.com
214-533-4964

AUTHOR

Ken Farmer didn't write his first full novel until he was sixty-nine years of age. He often wonders what the hell took him so long. At age seventy-seven…he's currently working on novel number twenty-five.

Ken spent thirty years raising cattle and quarter horses in Texas and forty-five years as a professional actor (after a stint in the Marine Corps). Those years gave him a background for storytelling…or as he has been known to say, "I've always been a bit of a bull---t artist, so writing novels kind of came naturally once it occurred to me I could put my stories down on paper."

Ken's writing style has been likened to a combination of Louis L'Amour and Terry C. Johnston with an occasional Hitchcockian twist…now that's a combination.

In addition to his love for writing fiction, he likes to teach acting, voice-over and writing workshops. His favorite expression is: "Just tell the damn story."

Writing has become Ken's second life: he has been a Marine, played collegiate football, been a Texas wildcatter, cattle and horse rancher, professional film and TV actor and now…a novelist. Who knew?

Ken Farmer's dialogue flows like a beautiful western river…it's the gold standard…Carole Beers

Web page: www.KenFarmer-Author.net

DEDICATION

This tome, is book #14 in the award-winning, The Nations Series and #4 of the spin-off Bone Series and is dedicated to one of mywriting inspirations, my long time buddy, star of stage, screen and television...**Alex Cord**.

Alex is also my visual inspiration for my character, Padrino, Bone's Godfather.

Alex told me once while I was writing my first book, 'Kenny, you'll never finish a book, you just have to walk away from it and start another. You can fiddle with it forever...just stop and move on.' Best advice I've ever had. You can never make it perfect.

ACKNOWLEDGMENT

The author gratefully acknowledges Lt. Colonel Clyde DeLoach, USMC (Ret.) and novelist Mary Deal for their invaluable help in proofing, beta reading and editing this novel. And a special Thank You to Vivian Jimenez Hall for gracing my cover and for being my visual inspiration for "Loraine".

TIMBER CREEK PRESS

CHAPTER ONE

SKEANS BOARDING HOUSE
GAINESVILLE, TEXAS

"What are you so nervous about, Bone?" asked Jack McGann.

Bone tugged at his starched collar. "Never did this before, Marshal."

"Neither had I, 'fore Angie an' me got hitched."

"Where did they perform your ceremony?"

"At Angie's house up in the Arbuckles, where we live now," said Jack. "But, I was more nervous about who was doin' it."

"Who was that?" asked Bone.

"The Judge…Judge Isaac Parker."

"Ooo, the Hanging Judge, see what you mean. Would have liked to met him. Heard he was a great man."

Marshal Lindsey nodded. "Passed away in '96, Brights disease…He could look right through you. Knowed when you were lyin', too."

Jack chuckled. "One time, he was tryin' this colored feller fer murder an' they found him guilty. So, the Judge sentenced him to hang an' the feller's attorney jumped up an' run up to protest to the Judge that the sentence was too harsh." Jack looked around at the other guests. "Well, the Judge jest pointed his finger at the man…That attorney, he fell to the floor almost in a state of apoplexy an' laid there till the Judge entered his chambers. Surprised he didn't piss his pants…Judge Parker never said a word to 'im…jest pointed his finger. You'd a thought he wuz God Almighty his self."

"Dang, that would have been a sight to see," said Bone as he looked over at the archway covered with branches from a female juniper, loaded with cones of ripe purple berries, and a large sprig of mistletoe hung from the center.

The area around the arch was permeated with the pleasant cedar smell from the juniper. It was placed in front of a number of wooden folding chairs with a center aisle between them.

Bone and Loraine's wedding was being held in Faye Skeans' green winter rye grass covered large back yard surrounded by walls of shrubbery. It was the same place where Sheriff Mason Flynn and Deputy US Marshal Fiona Mae Miller, Bone's great grand parents, were married the previous spring and Walt Durbin and Frances Ann Sullivant were married two years before that.

Doctor Winchester Ashalatubbi, also known by his Chickasaw tribal name of *Anompoli Lawa*—it means, He Who Talks to Many—was performing the ceremony in his capacity as a Doctor of Divinity, as he did for Mason and Fiona.

His credentials as a Doctor of Divinity were in addition to his degree as a physician and his position as the Shaman, or spiritual leader, of the Chickasaw tribe.

Jack has been know to say, 'Winchester can birth you, marry you, doctor you and your spirit, and bury you'.

Anompoli Lawa took his place in the center of the arch as Angie sang the wedding march to the accompaniment of Marshal Loss Hart on the fiddle. The doctor was dressed in a traditional beaded white doeskin war shirt of the Chickasaw Nation and held his worn, black leather covered Bible.

Loraine stepped out of the back door of Faye's three story, red brick, Queen Ann style house in a beautiful white satin gown, tight around her wasp waist with white ruffled Spanish lace around the top of her bodice and over her shoulders in a scoop-neck style. Jack and Angie's adopted daughter, ten year old Aurali Red, carried the dress's long train.

Bone had taken his place in front of and to Doctor Ashalatubbi's left. His knees almost buckled when he saw Loraine step out of the door.

Her lustrous long black hair shined in the late afternoon sun on this bright and clear fall day, only slightly enhanced with a small amount of brilliantine. It was done up in a Newport coiffure with a spiral bun on top of a French twist, held by pins, two pearl combs and a tall pearl encrusted Spanish comb in the front. The rest of Loraine's hair was in tight ring curls on both sides. It was pulled straight back from her forehead giving her a very aristocratic look. She was stunning.

Mason, acting as Bone's Best Man, leaned over to the big man. "Close your mouth, Bone, you'll catch flies."

"Oh, right."

"But, I don't blame you. Loraine could stop a war."

"Or start one," added Bone.

Loraine was being given away by the legendary Deputy US Marshal Bass Reeves, while Fiona Mae Flynn was her Matron of Honor.

The chairs were filled with a number of people from Gainesville, Jacksboro and the Nations. They included, Deputy US Marshal Selden Lindsey, Angie and Deputy US Marshal Jack McGann, with Baby Sarah. Cooke County Sheriff Walt Durbin and his wife Frances, with their toddler. Lisanne Gifford, Buster Martin and Slim Parker were also on one side of the aisle.

Texas Ranger Bodie Hickman, his wife Annabel and their twins, Bass and Cassie Ann, Mason's sister, Mary Lou and her husband, Cletus Wilson along with their adopted daughter, the diminutive stranded alien, Lucy. Deputy Gomer Platt and his intended Emma Lou Burke, and Lollie Whitaker from the stage with Loraine and Bone, were also on the other, along with some of Faye's friends and neighbors.

They all were turned in their chairs watching Loraine, Bass and Aurali Red step stately down the aisle to the music. Loraine carried a bouquet of purple aster flowers with a yellow center—similar to a daisy.

Loraine stopped in front of *Anompoli Lawa,* handed her flowers to Fiona and turned to face Bone.

Doctor Ashalatubbi began, "We are gathered here today in the sight of God, and the presence of friends and loved ones, to celebrate one of life's greatest moments. We are here to give recognition to the beauty of love that is shared between Bone and Loraine and as they complete their family in holy matrimony. Marriage is a contract not to be entered into lightly…"

He finished the invocation, the prayer and the exchange of vows, with the 'I do's', and then asked for the rings.

"May we now have the rings?"

Bodie and Annabel's twins, Bass and Cassie had walked up behind Loraine and Bone with tiny satin pillows. There was a plain gold band in the center of each.

"The ring, an unbroken circle, represents unending love. As often as either of you look upon these rings, may you be reminded of this moment and the love you have promised to one another. Darrell Ulysses Bone, please place this ring on Loraine's finger and repeat your commitments."

Bone looked deep into her limpid brown eyes. "Loraine, I give you this ring as a symbol of my love and that I'm choosing to share my life's journey with you. I give you this ring with the pledge to love you today, tomorrow, and always."

"Now, Loraine Maria Rodriguez, please place this ring on Bone's finger and repeat your commitments."

"Bone, I give you this ring as a symbol of my love and that I'm choosing to share my life's journey with you I give you this ring with the pledge to love you today, tomorrow, and always."

"Darrell and Loraine, I want to wish you both much love and happiness as you begin your new journey. Remember to keep lots of laughter in your life and love will never be far behind…"

"No problem there," muttered Loraine with a grin showing her perfect white teeth.

Winchester smiled, then continued, "Now Darrell and Loraine, you have pledged your faith to each other in the company of your family and friends.

"By the power vested in me by the State of Texas, I now pronounce you… husband and wife.

"Darrell Bone, you may now kiss your beautiful bride…Family and friends, I am proud to present for the first time as husband and wife…Mr. and Mrs. Bone."

Bone had showed Jack McGann how to use his smart phone to take pictures and he was taking one after another.

The six foot eight, Bone picked Loraine off the ground with his hands around her tiny waist, held her to him and kissed her, her feet dangling over a foot in the air. She had wrapped her arms around his neck and returned the kiss, curling her left leg up.

After a moment, *Anompoli Lawa* cleared his throat. Bone and Loraine broke their kiss, glanced at the venerable Shaman and both blushed. He set her down to the thunderous applause of the attendees.

"What's the matter, can't ya'll wait," commented Mason with a chuckle as he slapped Bone on the back.

The ladies all gathered around Loraine to give her a hug and well wishes while the men congratulated Bone. A stainless steel flask was soon produced and began making the rounds.

Lollie Whitaker, who helped Bone tend to a wounded Loraine on the stage and at Doctor Mosiers office, also hugged Loraine's neck and whispered in her ear, "See, I told you that you were both running from it, but, it was there and that you could run, but you couldn't hide from it…forever. That love was going to hit you and Bone one day…and hit you hard." She smiled.

Loraine kissed her cheek. "I didn't believe you, Lollie, but you were so right." She glanced over at Bone with the men.

Jack handed Bone his phone back and his stainless steel flask. "Took a bunch of pictures. That's an interesting gadget."

Bone took the phone and then flask and looked at Jack. "Appreciate it, Marshal…This isn't Cactus Wine, is it?"

Jack looked puzzled. "Since I have no idee what that is…No…This is good old Kentuck sour mash."

"Whew, good thing…Tell you about Cactus Wine sometime," Bone replied and turned the flask up.

"You got me interested, Bone, what is it?" asked Jack.

Bone grinned. "Tequila and peyote tea, bottled by the Souza family in Mexico."

Jack staggered back a step and grabbed his chest. "My God in Heaven."

You got that right," replied Bone.

Loraine walked over to Bone from talking with the ladies, jumped up, threw her arms around his neck and gave him a big kiss, and then leaned back.

"I can't believe I'm now going to be called,

'Missus Bone'…'Missus Bone, oh, my God…Who knew? Bone and Missus Bone…Guess it's going to be like, Mr. and Mrs. North."

"Except we're not amateur detectives, Missus Bone…we're professionals."

"True, Mister Bone," Loraine replied.

"Ya'll goin' any place for your honeymoon?" asked Mason.

"Bodie suggested San Antonio," said Bone looking at Loraine.

"I understand it's an interestin' place to relax, see the Alamo…an'…"

"What are you talking about, mister?" asked Mason's wife, Deputy US Marshal Fiona Flynn as she walked up.

"Just said I heard that San Antonio was a good place to go for a honeymoon…dear."

"Uh-huh. Why haven't we ever gone there?…Fact is, why haven't we ever gone anywhere for a honeymoon?"

"Uh…"

"Say, why don't ya'll go down there with us? We'll make it a double honeymoon." Bone looked down at Loraine again.

She smiled and nodded. “Some of my ancestors lived there.”

“Dang, Bone, why didn’t I think of that?”

Fiona’s steel-gray eyes drilled her husband. “I was thinking the exact same thing, Mister Flynn.”

“Well, Missus Flynn, would you like to take our long delayed honeymoon to San Antonio?”

She smiled. “Thought you’d never ask.”

“Ya’ll try to stay out of mischief, now,” cautioned Lucy, with a knowing smile.

§§§

CHAPTER TWO

SKEANS BOARDING HOUSE
GAINESVILLE, TEXAS

The photographer set up the tripod for his Henry Clay Dry Plate camera in front of the group of wedding attendees. His assistant sprinkled an appropriate amount of flash powder in his tray.

"All right, folks, on the count of three I want all of you to look at the camera and please don't move until I tell you. The tray Billy is holding above his head will flash, lighting our picture." He ducked under his black cover and made his final focus. "All right, now, One, Two, Three…Hold it."

He squeezed the rubber bulb in his hand, the flash powder exploded, sending a cloud of white smoke up into the overhanging limbs of the winter bare red oak above. "Keep holding…all right, you may relax…Think we got it."

"Say, Mister photographer, how about taking another one with all these famous law officers along with my family here? May not ever have them all together again," said Bone.

Everyone muttered their approval and started lining up. In the front row was Loraine, Lucy and Mary Lou. Behind them was Texas Ranger Bodie Hickman, Deputy US Marshal Jack McGann, Deputy US Marshal Selden Lindsey, Deputy US Marshal Loss Hart, Cooke County Sheriff Walt Durbin, Deputy Gomer Platt and Shaman *Anompoli Lawa*. The back row was Bone, Deputy US Marshal Bass Reeves, Deputy US Marshal Fiona Miller Flynn, and Jack County Sheriff Mason Flynn.

The photographer went through the same procedure and took the picture. "I think we got it."

"Might be worth something one day," said Bone with a grin. "Never can tell."

The lyrical strains of the William Tell Overture wafted across Faye's backyard at the same time the air shimmered like a heat wave for a couple of seconds.

Mason looked at Bone. "That comin' from your butt?"

"Uh...Yeah...Huh?" Bone reached to the back pocket of his suit pants and pulled out his smart phone that Lucy had given him in 2014.

"Bone," he answered with a questioning look on his face.

"Damn you, Bone! Where the hell are you?" yelled the Chief of Police of Gainesville PD, Captain St. John, from the speaker.

"Hey, Cap'n...You wouldn't believe...Hell, not sure I believe it myself. We're..." Bone's voice blared from St. John's speaker, and then abruptly stopped.

"What happened?" asked Corporal Stella Johnson, a gorgeous twenty-five year old blond investigator, in plain clothes, in the Gainesville PD sitting across the desk from the 5’8”, stocky black Captain in 2018. “Lose the connection?”

“Bone!...Bone, dammit.” He looked at the face of his Galaxy. “Gone...Shit.”

“He said ‘we’...Loraine must be with him,” said Stella.

“Yeah, but where?” St. John looked at Stella.

Patrolman Juan Gomez knocked on the door jam of the Chief’s office.

“Come,” said St. John.

The tall, slender Gomez stepped in the open doorway and laid a folder on St. John’s desk. “Found Bone’s Thing.”

“Beg your pardon?” the chief asked.

“His Thing...that 1971 Volkswagen Thing he was restoring.”

“Oh, right...right. Misunderstood what you were sayin’.”

Stella tried to hide a giggle.

St. John opened the folder and scanned it. “What in hell?” He looked up at Juan.

“Sheriff deputy from Palo Pinto County found it up at Possum Kingdom Lake...apparently abandoned...Had water in it from a couple of rains...Think they went fishin’ an’ drowned?”

"Not in this lifetime. Bone was a Force Recon Marine…about the same thing as a SEAL. Believe me, I know, I was in the Corps with him…His CO, actually," said St. John. "Never saw him in a situation he couldn't handle."

"Oh…Didn't know. Just makin' an observation…Sir."

"They tow it in to the county pound?" asked Stella.

"Yep. Said they'd throw a tarp on it an' hold it till Bone or somebody comes and gets it," said Gomez.

Bone looked at his screen. "Nothing. Huh…Had one bar for a few seconds, what the…"

"And the Captain called?…How?" asked Loraine.

Bone shook his head. "Damn if I know, hon."

Lucy looked up at the big man. "What's that instrument you have there, Bone? "Looks like a communicating device."

"It's a, what we call…uh, a smart phone…uh from our time. Has a lot of features besides just talking with someone. Can even do a video call…Hey, you actually gave me this one after you were rescued in 2014, Lucy…You added some stuff."

"Bone, keep your voice down. Not everyone here knows about where we came from," said Loraine, glancing around to see if anyone was listening.

"Oh…right, Pard." He turned back to Lucy and spoke sotto voce, "You put an app on it and some other stuff so we could communicate with you out in space at the 2nd Lagrangian point where you were, or will be, stationed as a Watcher…There was a tiny image of you in your formfitting gray space suit with the big black almond-shaped lenses for your eyes here on the screen as the icon…but, the app disappeared when we were transported back to 1898 in that cave."

"How could we get a call back in this time, Bone?" whispered Loraine.

"I think I can answer that," said Lucy softly. "The electromagnetic vortex wave that sent you here exists in numerous places all over your world and no one knows exactly how they're activated or where they all are…But, other than during the occurrence of the blue moon that *Anompoli Lawa* mentioned, we know they flux in and out for occasional short spurts and in various wave strengths…"

"So, Gainesville must be located at another one of those points like the cave we entered down on the Brazos?" Loraine said, interrupting the small pixie-haired alien woman.

Lucy nodded and continued, "…and apparently it just activated, weakly, for about nine seconds."

"This whole thing keeps getting weirder and weirder. Next thing you know, Cap'n St. John will appear out of thin air and start steady chewing on our asses, Pard."

"Nothing would surprise me anymore, baby," replied Loraine. "Don't know how anything could top you and I finding out we were in love." She linked her arm through his and leaned over to him. "I would have given that one chance in hell…Maybe not even that."

"Know what you mean, Pard, but I'm not complaining."

She stood on her tip toes and gave him a peck. "Me neither."

GAINESVILLE PD
2018

"Stella, you and Peach scoot down to Palo Pinto and go over Bone's Thing with a fine tooth comb…Uh, let's just say his Volkswagen from now on, shall we?"

Stella blushed and grinned. "Yes, sir."

"Anyway, ya'll go over there and check it out, and then go out to the lake where they found it…do the same out there…I want some answers. Somethin' very odd's goin' on here."

"Aye, aye, Cap'n…As you wish, Cap'n," she said getting to her feet.

"Don't push it, Corporal or you'll be back on patrol duty," St. John said.

Stella grinned again, picked up the folder and headed out of his office down to the forensics lab.

She stopped by the lounge and got two cups of coffee on the way.

Stella opened the door of the forensics lab and saw Peach Presley in a white lab coat, bent over, looking through a 40X-2000X High Power Trinocular Compound Microscope.

"Hey, Peach," Stella said.

BONE & LORAINE

The tall, attractive brunette, from Georgia, looked over at the door. "Hey, Stella, just give me a minute, honey."

"No prob…Brought you a cup of shellac."

"How old is it?" she asked, without looking up from the microscope.

"Yesterday…I think."

"Umm, should be just about right, then." She looked up and massaged the bridge of her nose. "I swear, my eyes feel like two burnt holes in a blanket," Peach said in her heavy Georgia accent.

Stella handed her the white porcelain cup with a Colt .45 semiautomatic and a Lone Star Shooting Supply logo on the side.

"Bless your heart, Stella." Peach blew across the top and took a sip, shook and closed one eye. "This may put hair on your chest," she wheezed.

"Pass," answered Stella, grinning. "We gotta make a trip and do some work."

"Oh, my goodness, now what?"

"As you know, Bone and Loraine are missin', but the captain got him on his cell just a little bit ago for about eight or nine seconds, so we know he's all right and that Loraine is with him on account he said, 'we'."

"Bless their hearts."

"Any chance you can trace the Captain's call an' find out where Bone and Loraine are?" asked Stella.

Peach grinned and shook her head. "That's only on NCIS, besides if there is that type of equipment, we couldn't afford it anyways…Wish I had what's in Abby's lab."

"Yeah, heard that…If wishes and wants were feathers and wings, a frog wouldn't bump his ass every time he hops…We're lucky to get new squad cars every five years from the county."

"Uh-huh…Now, we gotta do what?"

"The Palo Pinto Sheriff's Department found his Thing…"

Peach inhaled sharply. "Bone lost his thing? Bless his heart."

"No, no, his Volkswagen Thing."

"Oh, thank goodness." She fanned her face with her right hand. "Bone's too hot to lose his thing."

Stella shook her head and closed her eyes for a moment, and then looked back up at Peach. She was 5'2" and Peach was 5'10". The rest of the department called them Mutt and Jeff II…Bone and Loraine were Mutt and Jeff I, with his 6'8" and her 5'3".

"The captain wants us to go to Palo Pinto and give it a good going over, and then go up to Possum Kingdom where they found it and look around."

"You mean from rear-ends to elbows?"

"Somethin' like that. When can you be ready to go?" asked Stella.

"Oh, honey, what time is it."

"Eleven thirty-two."

"You waitin' on me you're backin' up, girl."

"Grab your gear, then…Meet you in the parkin' lot…we'll take the black plain wrapper." Stella turned and headed down to her office.

SKEANS BOARDING HOUSE
1898

Bone and Loraine, along with Mason and Fiona sat in the parlor of Faye's boarding house having afternoon coffee. Everyone else had already headed back home except for the ones that lived in Gainesville.

Bodie and Annabel walked in from the stairway, through the foyer, each carrying one of the twins.

They set them down on the floor as soon as they entered.

Faye came through the large dining room from the kitchen with two more cups of coffee. “Heard ya’ll comin’ down the stairs.” She handed each a steaming cup.

“Thanks, Faye, you make the best coffee…”

Annabel elbowed Bodie in the ribs.

“Oh…Uh, next to yours, sweetheart,” he stammered.

“It’s a good thing you caught yourself, Bodie,” she said, and then turned and winked at Faye.

She winked back. “I’ll bring some of Loraine and Bone’s lemon wedding cake in just a moment,” Faye said as she turned around and headed back to the kitchen.

“Cain’t believe ya’ll are sittin’ in the parlor instead of up in your room on the day of your weddin’,” commented the ranger.

“Bodie Hickman!”

“Well…”

“It’s all right, Annabel, we were trying to figure out where we could stay down in San Antonio,” said Loraine.

"Well, I was stationed there before the Rangers sent me up here an' I would recommend the Villa de la Vega. It's down close to the river and about two blocks from the Alamo. It's a lot like Faye's here…Lots of good places to eat down there, too" replied Bodie. "I know the proprietor, Sophia de la Vega…the widow of Don Felipe Diego de la Vega…I stayed there."

"Don Felipe Diego de la Vega?" questioned Loraine, sitting up quickly. "My great great great grandfather was a Don Felipe Diego de la Vega in San Antonio…My, my."

"Small world," said Bone.

"He was married twice. His first wife, my third great grandmother, died of cholera in 1860…then he married a twenty year old Castilian, Sophia Garza, in '65…That has to be her."

"When did he pass away?" asked Fiona.

"In '90 at the age of seventy-five…heart failure, my grandmother said."

"More and more reasons why we were sent back to this time. That makes her your third great step grandmother," said Bone. "I say that sounds like a good place to me."

"There is one thing," said Bodie.

"That would be?" asked Mason.

"There have been six suicides there since Sophia turned it into a rooming house."

"Say, what if maybe the villa is even haunted…Mua-ha-ha-ha-ha." Bone laughed in his worst imitation of Bela Lugosi.

"Damn you, Bone, that's not funny," commented Loraine.

"Don't throw it, this is Faye's good china we're drinking coffee from." He grinned and winked at her.

"What am I going to do with you?"

"Well, I've got three suggestions, darlin', and the first two don't count." He wiggled his eyebrows at her.

She blushed. "We'll see…If you play your cards right, mister."

"You got to know when to hold 'em, know when…"

"Please don't ruin that song, Bone, it's one of my favorites of Kenny Rogers," said Loraine.

"Yes, dear."

§§§

CHAPTER THREE

VILLA DE LA VEGA
SAN ANTONIO, TEXAS

An ornate sign in the rock and cactus front yard read:

VILLA de la VEGA Rooming House.

Vernon Wyland and Clayton Armstrong were playing chess on one side of a shaded arbor in the open center garden of the large, two story, square stucco adobe Spanish style hacienda with a red tile roof. There was a six foot wide balcony that ran around the outside of the hacienda at the second floor, as well as around on the inside, overlooking the interior garden.

The chess set was carved from solid white and black onyx with a matching white and a black onyx chess board that was owned by Don Flipe Deigo de la Vega, who had it carved for him in Mexico.

The present owner of Villa de la Vega, his widow, Sophia de la Vega, of Castilian Spanish heritage, sat off to the side in a rocking chair, watching the two men and enjoying a glass of ice tea.

It was believed that onyx, especially black, absorbed and transformed negative energy. Black onyx is said to aid the development of emotional and physical strength as well as stamina.

"There you go Clayton…Check."

"Hell, Vernon, don't think it will make any difference." Clayton grinned and moved his knight. "Checkmate."

"Well, I'll be dipped…That's four straight games you've won, Clay. Thought I had you that time."

"Yeah, sorry about that Vern. You're a pretty good chess player, but I guess I should have told you...I'm a Master. I apologize...Damn, but, I don't know when I've had more fun."

Vernon finished off his iced tea. "Glad you've enjoyed yourself."

Clayton picked up his empty tea glass and looked at it. "Think I'm gonna go upstairs and take a little nap before Anita gets back from shopping." He got up, glass in his hand and started toward one of the doors from the garden that led inside.

"You can just leave the glass, Mister Armstrong, I'm headed to the kitchen anyway."

"Thank you, Sophia," Clayton said.

"If you need anything, just give the bell pull a yank. Remember, your room is three pulls," replied Sophia.

"Yes, Ma'am." He opened the door and went inside.

Vernon, a weathered forty-five year old veteran cavalry soldier of the Indian wars, got to his feet also and followed Clayton. "Guess I'll go ahead and fill the lamps in the upstairs hall, Ma'am."

"Thank you, Vernon."

She also got up walked over to the chess table, picked up Clayton and Vernon's tea glasses and headed to the door.

Sophia entered the kitchen carrying the empty glasses. She dumped the remaining ice from the glasses into the wet sink, washed the glasses and put them on a towel upside down on the cabinet top to dry.

She walked over to the wood-burning cook stove to stir a big pot of marinara sauce with a wooden spoon.

Vernon walked into the kitchen, stepped over to the ice box and took out a fried chicken leg and had a big bite.

"Don't ruin your supper, Vernon."

He sniffed of the marinara sauce on the stove and a big grin spread across his face. "Not much chance of that, Miz de la Vega."

The bell in the rack over against the far interior wall from Clayton Armstrong's room, rang once and stuck in the sideways position. Sophia and Vernon looked over at the bell.

"Oh, I thought I told you to fix that, Vernon."

"Did, Ma'am…Brand new rope inside the velvet sheath." He walked over to the bell and tried to return it to its down position, but it was stuck.

"Go on up and see if Mister Armstrong needs anything."

"Yes, Ma'am." He exited the door to the hall.

Vernon climbed the light red varnished adobe brick tile covered stairway with the hand-carved railing and walked down the hallway to the Armstrong's room and knocked.

There was no response. He knocked again. Nothing.

"Mister Armstrong, you in there?"

Vernon tried the brass door lever. It was locked. He knelt down to try to look in the keyhole. There was a key inserted in the lock from the other side. He knocked once more.

"Mister Armstrong?"

Sophia had heard Vernon trying to raise Clayton Armstrong from downstairs, topped the stairway and approached Vernon.

Is there a problem?"

He frowned. "Don't know, Ma'am. He doesn't answer and the door's locked from the inside."

Push the key out and use your master skeleton key.

Vernon took out a long thin screwdriver from his tool pouch, knelt down again and pushed the key out the other side. There was a clink as the brass key hit the hardwood floor. He inserted his master skeleton key and unlocked the door. Vernon turned the lever, pushed the door open and looked inside.

He dropped to his knees as he stared in the room and made a moaning cry from deep in his throat.

Sophia stepped closer and put her hand on his shoulder. “What is it, Vernon?”

He could only point inside the Armstrong room.

Sophia looked inside the partially open solid walnut carved door.

Clayton Armstrong was hanging by his neck from the bell pull against the back wall next to the bed. His feet were twelve inches from the floor and tied together with a dark green window drapery sash. There was a piano stool next to his dangling feet. Clayton Armstrong was dead.

Sophia screamed and fainted in the hallway next to Vernon who was still on his knees.

SKEANS BOARDING HOUSE

I'll go downtown and send a telegram, reserving two suites at the villa and I'll check on the train schedules…Should be a straight shot through Ft. Worth," said Mason.

"I'll go with you. Miz De La Vega knows me. I'll tell her ya'll ain't gonna trash the place…You're house broke."

"Are you speaking from experience, Bodie?" asked Loraine.

"Me?"

"I don't see anyone else in here from San Antonio, Ranger," said Fiona.

Mason grinned and glanced at the others. "We takin' our mounts?"

"I don't think we'll be chasing outlaws on the scout. Let's leave them home. We can rent a carriage there to get around," commented Fiona. "Besides Doctor Mosier would frown on it in my condition."

"Do believe I'm taking my hand cannon and a box of ammo, though. Like I always say…never leave home without it…and plenty ammo," said Bone.

"Gotta agree with that," added Mason.

"Better to be safe than sorry," commented Loraine.

"We'd have been up the creek if you hadn't had it at my funeral," said Flynn.

"True," added Fiona.

PALO PINTO, TEXAS
2018

Stella and Peach are scouring Bone's Thing in the county impound yard.

"Find anything, Peach," asked Stella.

"Nothing out of the norm for Bone, bless his heart. His prints and Loraine's…Gum and candy wrappers. Sonic sacks and left over fries…you know?…My goodness, a couple of these fries are petrified." She held one up and tapped it on the dash. It sounded like a limb from a tree.

"Yeah. doesn't surprise me…I suspect they were goin' fishin' at Possum Kingdom."

"With Loraine? I declare, honey, figured the only way she liked fish was from Tom Thumb's…The last time he took her out to show her how to hunt squirrels, she got madder'n a wet hen."

"Why?" asked Stella.

"Got mud on her shoes."

"Shut up."

Peach giggled. "Bone's funny as all get out…Think he led her through a bog on account she wore shoes instead of boots."

"Why didn't she just talk to him about it, instead of gettin' mad and all."

"She'd be better off talkin' to a fence post. Bone listens worst than anybody I know…She knows him. They been workin' together for four years."

"You'd think she had him figured out by now," said Stella as she packed up her kit.

"Bone could confuse the horns off a billy goat," replied Peach as she snapped her case shut.

"Ask me, I think they're in love…Just don't know it."

"Hush your mouth, girl."

"Let's head on out to the lake…Bring your bathin' suit?" asked Stella.

Peach tilted her head forward toward Stella and arched her brows. "Do what?…I figured we'd just go skinny dippin', if the water wadn't too cold when we're done. Honey, that water's clear as a bell, you know?"

"Works for me."

Thirty minutes later they drove up to the location where the deputy found Bone's Thing and parked the black squad car.

"Any idea what we're lookin' for?" asked Peach.

"Anything that doesn't belong an' looks like Bone or Loraine."

"Easy for you to say."

They worked their way over to the cliff edge overlooking the water.

"This would be a good spot to cast out in the channel," said Stella.

Peach nodded. "Bone doesn't strike me as the type to go fishin' with a cane pole an' a bobber."

"You think?"

"I'll betcha a storm came up and they took cover somewhere because there's no top on his Thing, uh, Volkswagen," said Peach. "Can't believe Bone likes it…it's so tee-niny."

"You are talkin' about the Volkswagen aren't you?"

"Lord have mercy, honey, I hope so." Peach giggled.

"Isn't that a cave up there on that ridge?" asked Stella.

"Let's go up there an' take a looky-see," suggested Peach.

"Thought you'd never bring it up."

"I'm gonna slap the mess out of you." Peach grinned at her best friend.

They climbed up to the entrance, each took out their tac lights and shined them around the opening.

"Look, see those tracks just inside the entrance? Big ones an' little ones." Stella glanced at Peach. "Bone and Loraine?"

"If it's not, they're gonna miss a dang good chance."

"Notice one thing about 'em though?" asked Stella.

"What do you mean?"

"There are tracks goin' in…" Stella looked at Peach. "…but none leavin'."

"Well, well, now, don't that beat all?"

They cast their beams to the back and saw the cave closed down to nothing.

“Not very deep an’ no openin’ in the back,” commented Peach.

“Uh-huh…Shine your light all over, especially in the corners and around rocks for rattlesnakes,” said Stella.

“Ooo…I hate spiders an’ snakes.”

“All the more reason to look closely. Gettin’ a little late in the year…’Magine most of them are already denned up underground somewhere.”

“Isn’t this underground?…Oh, look, somebody built a fire next to the wall over there. Doesn’t look too old, either.” Peach knelt down and stirred the ashes with her finger. “Still loose.” She looked around. I’d say they burned up all the available wood.”

“Looks like they were in here for a spell…Both sat down there.” Stella pointed.

“Uh-huh…” Peach rubbed her arms. “My goodness, look at the hairs on my arms…They’re standin’ straight up.”

“Mine too…What’s that on the wall there?”

Peach shined her flashlight up about head high.

"Petroglyphs…Ancient Native American, my guess…Let's get some pictures and take them to Bone's godfather, Padrino. If anyone knows what they mean…he will," commented Stella.

§§§

CHAPTER FOUR

SANTA FE DEPOT
GAINESVILLE, TEXAS
1898

Bodie and Mason walked inside the Western Union Telegraph and Cable office in the Santa Fe Depot. They approached the clerk on the other side of the counter.

"Need to send a couple of telegrams, pard," said Mason.

"Yes, sir," replied the young clerk that had replaced Percy Gilhooley who had been killed by Calvin Mankiller when he and other outlaws robbed the horse race taking place at the Cooke County Fair Grounds a couple of years earlier.

"Let's just send one, Sheriff, I'll write a note to Sophia, tellin' her ya'll are comin' down and need two suites…plus say howdie," said Bodie.

"Ya'll sheriff deputies?" asked the slight built agent with awe.

"He's the County Sheriff of Jack County and I'm a Texas Ranger," replied Bodie.

"Gollygee whizbang! A High Sheriff an' a Texas Ranger in here. My girlfriend ain't gonna believe it." He slid the note pad over to Bodie. "Just put what you need to say, Ranger, an' I'll get it right out…My name's Marvin Clearwater."

"That the latest train schedule south through Ft. Worth to San Antonio?" Mason pointed to a slate board with the train times.

"Yes, sir, Sheriff. The train that goes through here, the Gulf and Colorado, on the way to Corpus

Christi, stops in San Antonio. No need to change trains atall."

"Thanks for the information, Marvin…What's the arrival time in San Antonio if the train leaves Gainesville on time?"

"It's a eighteen hour trip, Sheriff…countin' stops an' all." He looked back at the board. "She's scheduled to get here at four ten this afternoon from Oklahoma City, so, all goes well, she should pull in to San Antonio at ten tomorrow mornin'."

Mason nodded at Bodie. "Put that in your message, Bodie."

"Right."

He filled out the text for the telegram and pushed the pad back over when he was finished. "There you go, Marvin."

"Are you goin' to wait for a reply, Ranger?"

"Nope, just send it over to Miz Skeans Boardin' House, if you would," said Bodie.

"Yes, sir, I can handle that. The messenger is on a run right now, but should be back any minute. Send him right over with any reply."

"Thank you, Marvin." Bodie laid a Morgan silver dollar on the counter.

Bodie and Mason both tipped their hats as they opened the door and headed back to their horses tied up to iron hitching posts at the curb.

As they rode over to California Street on the way to Lindsey Street, Mason turned to Bodie just before they made the corner

"Where's the nearest livery where we can rent a carriage?"

"Would you believe right next door to the villa," replied Bodie. "Got some nice baroques there."

BONE'S RANCH
COOKE COUNTY, TEXAS
2018

Stella put the plain black squad car in park after she stopped in front of Bone's period ranch house. The house and surrounding section of land was deeded to Bone by Lucy when she was rescued in 2014, for saving her life.

Lucy had inherited it from her adoptive parents, Mason Flynn's sister, Mary Lou and her husband, Cletus Wilson.

Bone's godfather, Padrino, was sitting on the wide wraparound porch of the white, shiplap, late 1800s, dog-run style ranch house, in a slat-backed rocking chair. The house had a new standing-seam green metal roof. Lucy's dog, Tyrin, sat beside him.

"Get out, ladies," the seventy year old 'Nam' vet, Marine welcomed them, getting up from the chair.

The muscular blond and white pit bull jumped up and down, wiggling all over in joy at seeing the girls again.

"Hi, Padrino," Stella said as she gave the wiry, white-haired man a hug.

Peach followed suit.

They both knelt down and hugged Tyrin and were rewarded with kisses.

"How am I so blessed to have such lovely ladies come all the way out here to see an old man?"

"It's about Bone, Padrino," Stella replied.

"I know…I mean, I don't know where he is either…Come on inside, I put the coffee pot on just before I came out. Should be ready by now."

"Bless your sweet heart, Padrino, that sounds wonderful," said Peach.

"You ladies had lunch?"

They exchanged looks.

"No, but it's all right," responded Stella.

"Nonsense, I smoked a ham out in the smoker yesterday. It's so tender, you don't need a knife, I just pull the meat off with a fork…Let's make some sandwiches. What do you say?"

"That's so sweet, Padrino, I could sit still for that," said Peach.

"You can tell me what it was about Bone that brought ya'll all the way out here while I make the sandwiches…Got some fresh bone bread I made yesterday."

"Bone has his own bread?" asked Stella.

Padrino chuckled. "No, honey, it's a New York deli, Italian type bun…hard crust, real flavorful and chewy. Great for po-boys."

"Sounds scrumptious," said Peach.

Padrino pulled a large Tupperware container that was full of smoked ham chunks, mustard, stacker pickles and muenster cheese from the fridge and got three of the bone bread buns from the keeper. He set it all on the counter and got his bread knife out to slice the buns in half.

"Well, it all started when the captain tried to reach Bone on his cell for the umpteenth time this morning…and would you believe it…Bone answered," said Stella.

Padrino looked up and cocked his head. "Go on." He pitched Tyrin a chunk of ham that he caught before it hit the original hardwood floor…

Ten minutes later, Stella and Peach had filled Padrino in and he had just set the huge po-boys, piled high with ham and two slices of cheese, in front of them on napkins.

Why don't we take these sandwiches, go into the office, plug your phone into the computer and take a good look at those petroglyphs, while we eat…Shall we?"

"Works for me," said Stella as she and Peach followed Padrino into his office carrying their sandwiches and coffee.

They didn't know that it was Lucy's bedroom when Mary Lou and Cletus were still alive.

He plugged Stella's smart phone into his computer with a USB cord and pulled up her photo gallery while they ate.

"That's a bison. That symbol there means a river…most likely the Brazos and that's an electrical storm…See the lightning?…Umm, interesting." He glanced over at the girls. "These petroglyphs are at least ten thousand years old maybe closer to fifteen," he said.

"My goodness, how on earth can you tell?" asked Peach.

He pointed at one of the carvings. "This is a petroglyph of a *Mammut Americanum*, the American mastodon…a distant relative of the elephant. They roamed the North American continent during the last ice age, which ended about ten thousand years ago."

"Well butter my butt and call me a biscuit…So this was their stompin' grounds?" asked Peach.

Padrino nodded. "All the way down to central Mexico…It's believed that they were hunted to their extinction by the Amerindians."

"What's that?" asked Stella as she pointed to a human-like figure with a large head.

"That, my dear, is, in my opinion…an alien."

"No way," said Peach.

"Well, we all met Lucy, so we know they do, in fact, exist and have been visiting our world for eons…In that petroglyph, however, the alien, while similar to what Lucy looks like in her space suit…you know the gray alien look…is different."

"Yes, we saw her, or a hologram of her in it after she was rescued," commented Stella.

"Uh-huh…But, see, this one is much taller than her race," added Padrino.

"I swani, it's a different race of aliens then?" asked Peach.

"In my opinion."

"What is that spiral?" inquired Stella.

"Well, that, according to the ancient alien theorists, is a symbol for a portal."

"Portal?" questioned Peach.

"An opening to another world, dimension…or time."

"Get out of town!" exclaimed Stella jumping to her feet. "No, wait, that's the only answer."

Padrino nodded. "Also, according to certain physicists as well as the ancient alien theorists, traveling to other worlds, dimensions or times is possible, and was done, through portals…It is believed that the open-ended spiral signifies the location of one of these ancient portals.

"They are known to be located all over the world. This theory was first promulgated by Nicola Tesla when he explained that an electromagnetic vortex wave anchored by certain gravitational anomalies can create a warp, or hole, in the folds of the fabric of time and space."

"Kinda like a star-gate on SG-1," said Stella.

Padrino grinned. "Something like that…and if they took refuge in that cave because of a storm…let's look at the lightning carving and the open-ended spiral along with no other exit…I'm afraid the inescapable conclusion is the vortex was activated by a lightning strike close by. Drawn there by the gravitational anomaly, and they were whisked away to another time…sort of like Edgar Rice Burroughs' character, John Carter, in a *Princess of Mars*…He was transported to another world…as well as another time."

"Oh, Lordy, Lordy, this is deeper'n granny's well," muttered Peach.

"According to a quote by Sherlock Holmes, or actually Author Conan Doyle…'Once you eliminate the impossible, whatever remains, no matter how improbable, must be the truth.'," added Padrino.

Stella and Peach exchanged glances.

"The captain will pitch a hissy fit with a tail on it if we go back and tell him that," said Peach as she held her head in both hands.

Tyrin put one paw on her knee, and then his chin.

“Maybe not. How about I go back into town with you and explain it to him?...He knows me and Lucy, so it shouldn’t be so hard...There really is no other explanation,” said Padrino.

“It’s just like a crime scene...We lay out the facts, show the captain the pictures, Padrino tells him that physics stuff...let him draw his own conclusion...and keep our butts out of the meat grinder,” added Stella.

Tyrin looked at Padrino and cocked his head.

§§§

CHAPTER FIVE

SKEANS BOARDING HOUSE
1898

Bone, Mason and Bodie were in the parlor having an afternoon touch of sour mash. The ladies were upstairs packing for the trip.

"Anyone need a freshen?" Bodie asked, holding up the amber cut glass decanter.

"Just a touch," said Mason, holding out his glass.

"I'm good," added Bone. "That Cactus Wine spoiled me. Got to see if I can find some down in San Antonio."

"Shouldn't be a problem there," commented Bodie. "Didn't you say it was tequila and peyote tea?"

"I did and believe me…"

A knock sounded from the front door. Mason, already standing near the roaring fireplace, set his glass on the mantle.

"I got it." He strode over to the foyer and the front door.

He opened it and greeted the Western Union messenger on the front porch. "Come on in, son, where it's warm."

"Thank you, sir." The teenager snatched the Western Union short-billed cap from his head. "Got a telegram here for Ranger Hickman," he said as he entered the foyer.

"He's in there…The big ugly redheaded one," said Mason.

"I heard that," came Bodie's voice from the parlor.

Mason grinned and led the messenger into the warm parlor.

"Here you are, sir." He handed the yellow envelope to Bodie and received a fifty cent piece in return. "Wow, thank you, Ranger…Should I wait for an answer?"

"Let's see, shall we?" He opened the envelope and took the thin yellow flimsy out and unfolded it. "From Sophia, 'Your suites are reserved and there will be someone to pick you up at the train station'…Well, well, this is interesting."

"You going to make us wait all day or just keep it to yourself?" proffered Bone.

"No, no." He looked over at Bone and Mason. "It seems that a guest at the villa committed suicide last week."

"Ooo, that's too bad," said Mason.

"That's not the point." He looked up again. "Sophia says something just isn't right. The guest was in a very good mood just moments before the apparent suicide. Wants me to come down and investigate."

"Well?" questioned Mason.

"Just can't, boys, I have to testify at a rustler's trial in the morning. I'll just send her an answer that all ya'll are more than capable of conducting an investigation."

"The girls are going to love this," muttered Flynn.

"We're going to be there, Mason, and you have to agree, this is what we do, besides, like Bodie says, he has to testify and there's no telling how long a trial is going to take."

"Good point, Bone," said Mason and nodded to Bodie.

"Take this, son…Sophia, impossible for me to come…stop. The two couples I made reservations for are all top law officers, two detectives, one sheriff and a US Deputy Marshal…stop. You are in good hands…stop. Texas Ranger Bodie Hickman…End." He handed the messenger another fifty cent piece.

"Yes, sir! Thank you, sir…get this right out." He looked in awe at Bone and Mason, nodded and headed back to the door.

After the boy had left, Bodie turned to Bone and Mason. "Wish Annabel and me could go with ya'll, I think you're going to have fun. Just so you know…That suicide?…Makes seven in the villa since Don Flipe Deigo de la Vega died…all by hanging."

"You're joking," commented Bone.

"Joke you not. Six…now seven suicides in the Villa de la Vega in eight years."

"Sounds like a Poe or Doyle mystery," said Fiona as she and Loraine stepped into the parlor from the foyer followed in a moment by Annabel.

"I have a feeling we're not going to be bored," added Loraine.

"You think?" replied Bone. He looked over at Loraine. "Don't forget to pack our crime scene kit, *Acushla*."

She cocked her head. "What's *Acushla*?"

Bone grinned. "It's a Gaelic word meaning…pulse of my heart."

"Aww," Loraine and Fiona said simultaneously.

Loraine grabbed his collar and pulled his head down to her level and planted a big kiss on his lips," and said, "I love you, too, big guy."

"Where did you hear that?" asked Fiona.

"It was something Lollic Whitaker said while Loraine was still out…She said Loraine was my *acushla*…" He kissed her back. "…and she was right."

"Awright, ya'll go back upstairs if you're goin' to start foolin' 'round," quipped Mason.

"You could take a lesson or two at that, Mister Flynn," said Fiona.

"Come here, woman." He grabbed the raven-haired beauty's arm and pulled her over against him and kissed her tenderly.

"Ooo, maybe we should be the ones to go back upstairs," she said and kissed him back.

"We may not get much work done down in San Antonio," commented Bone.

"And that's a problem because?" questioned Loraine.

"Well, we may have to come up for air once in a while," said Bone, pulling Loraine down onto his lap.

"Is that sour mash bourbon I smell?" asked Fiona.

"Yes, dear, would you like a glass?" answered Mason.

"Better make it a short one, Fiona. They've found out in our time that regular excessive alcohol is harmful to the baby," commented Loraine.

"Oh, maybe I'll just have some lemonade, then," she said as she headed toward the kitchen.

"I don't have such a problem...yet," said Loraine with a twinkle in her eye. "I'll take a small glass, please and thank you." She looked over at Mason.

"Yes, m'lady, comin' right up." He took one of the glasses from the cut glass set in Faye's bar hutch against the wall, filled it halfway and handed it to her.

"When I said a small glass, I didn't mean half a small glass."

"Oops." Flynn stepped back over to the dry bar and finished filling her glass and took it back over to her.

"That's more like it." Loraine took a small sip, like you should with quality liquor. "Mmm, that is smooth."

"Double-aged five years in charred white oak barrels or casks after being started with leftovers from a previous batch, much like sourdough bread," Mason answered. "Ya'll know that if it's not distilled in Bourbon County, Kentucky, it can't be called Bourbon whiskey?"

"Mexican law states that the fermented juice from the blue agave must come from the state of

Jalisco before it can be called tequila," added Bodie.

"Are we going to be graded on the curve for the quiz?" asked Bone as he took a sip of his sour mash bourbon.

"Well, I for one like to the know the history of my favorite drinks like Old Jake Beam Sour, started in 1795. It's smooth as silk," commented Fiona as she took a drink of her lemonade.

"That happens to be what the rest of ya'll are drinking," said Faye as she came through the door from the kitchen through the dining room.

"Well, it's certainly good, madam," said Bone. He turned to Loraine. "We all packed, my *Acushla*?"

"What does that mean, Bone?" Faye looked at the big man.

"It's Irish for 'pulse of my heart'," answered Fiona before Bone could start.

Faye took a sharp intake of a breath and put her hand to her bosom. "I think that's the most romantic thing I've ever heard."

"And to think it came from Bone." Mason took a sip of his sour mash.

Fiona glanced at him. “You could take some lessons on that, too, husband.”

Faye looked at Fiona and Mason. “ I think ya’ll are doin’ all right.”

“I’ll have to agree with you, Faye.” Fiona stepped over and hugged Mason. “He’ll do.”

Mason gave her a kiss and patted her shapely behind.

She looked over at him. “Later.”

“Won’t be any later until tomorrow. We have to catch that train…” He glanced at Faye’s grandfather clock on the far wall. “…in forty-five minutes.”

“Oh, speaking of, I made ya’ll a basket of food to take along with you for that long ride on the train…Fried chicken, roast beef sandwiches, fresh bread, watermelon rind preserves, pickles…”

Fiona interrupted, “Oh, good.”

Faye grinned and nodded. “…a couple of jars of tea…sweetened, and with a sprig of mint, plus wedding cake.”

“Oh, Faye that’s so sweet,” said Annabel.

“Not really. Have to get rid of that cake before I eat it all and have to let my dresses out.”

“Oh, hush up. You look fine.”

“You packed our extra ammo, right?”

Loraine looked at Bone with her 'I'm going to hurt you' look.

Bone nodded. "Figured."

"Then why'd you ask, you big lug?"

"Uh…"

"We better bring our bags down. Bodie, you want to help me harness up Big Red and Bart to the carriage?"

"May as well, before I'm the one gettin' in trouble." He grinned at Bone.

The big man set his empty glass down on its doily. "I'll help, too."

Fiona drained the last of her lemonade and got to her feet. "Cowards."

ROSA'S CANTINA
SAN ANTONIO

Vernon sat at a table over next to the far wall in the dim lit Mexican saloon. He had a bottle of mescal in front of him—it was half empty. He held a bar glass—both hands wrapped around it. His eyes were bloodshot.

The proprietor, Rosa Gomez, walked over to his table and leaned over. "Don't you think you've had enough, *Señor* Vernon?"

He slowly shook his head. "Ain't never enough, Rosa…not…not in the whole world…ain't enough." He picked up his glass with both hands and took a long drink, and then set it down. Both his hands shook.

"Let me get Sancho to help you back to the hacienda?"

Vernon shook his head again. "Don't live there no more," he slurred.

"Where do you live, *Señor*?"

He took another drink. "Nowhere…I don't live nowhere."

"You no at villa?" asked Rosa.

Vernon shook his head as his eyes filled. "Can't go back there." He paused and took a deep breath. "Can't never go back there…Ghosts."

§§§

CHAPTER SIX

GAINESVILLE PD
2018

"…and this symbol is generally recognized around the world as a symbol of some type of portal," commented Padrino, pointing to Captain St. John's monitor. "Just what kind…is open to conjecture."

"So you're saying that there was a brief opening or fold this morning with me and wherever the hell Bone and Loraine are?"

"Or whenever...That's the way I see it, David. Considering what my research into wave theory and electromagnetic vortexes has shown. That spiral there...I believe is open-ended to show that time continues and that you can cross from concentric ring inward to another concentric ring and theoretically...go back in time." Padrino paused and glanced at the captain, and then the girls. "Could be a prime example of Einstein's theory of special relativity where he explained quantum entanglement."

"Oh, I've read about that. He called it 'spooky action at a distance'," Peach spoke up.

"Exactly," said Padrino. "He also said the past, present, and future could all exist at the same time...I think your reaching Bone on your cell phone is a prime example of that."

St. John rubbed his temples and shook his head. "Only Bone."

"How did he sound, with the few words you were able to hear?" asked Padrino.

The captain looked up. “Happy…He sounded happy…When he answered, it was like he was surprised for a second, and then when he realized it was me…he sounded happy as a kid in a candy store when he said, ‘Hey, Cap’n…You wouldn’t believe…Hell, not sure I believe it myself. We’re’…and the connection was gone, no static, no chatter…Just one second he was there…and the next, he wasn’t.”

“That’s true. I heard him, too. Sounded like he had just won the lottery,” added Stella.

St. John spun his chair around and stared out the window for a moment and then turned back. “You don’t think this is one of his pranks, do you?…I mean if he can put two shotgun shells of flash powder in my ash tray and damn near blow the place up when the sheriff stubbed out his cigar…”

Stella and Peach both giggled.

“Bless Sheriff Brennan’s heart…Burnt all the hair off his right arm and his eyebrows, too…All we could hear down the hall, through the smoke, was him screamin’, ‘Damn you, Bone, you burnt me up!’” said Peach.

“Had to take him to the hospital…Eyebrows still haven’t grown back,” added Stella.

Padrino grinned and nodded. “Told me all about it when he got home. I think he giggled for two days.”

“Bone can’t hide anything, especially when he’s happy,” said St. John. “Was that way in the Corps over in Afghanistan, too.” He nodded again. “So, I don’t think he and Loraine are in any trouble…That I know.”

“Unless they kill each other…Bless their hearts, they’re like a cat and a dog.” Peach giggled again. “When they start snappin’ at each other, I have a dyin’ duck fit.”

St. John wrinkled his forehead. “Peach, what the hell does that mean?”

“Means I run an’ hide…an’ just listenin’ to them snipe at one another?…Well, honey, I get lost as last year’s Easter egg.”

St. John nodded and closed his eyes. “Know the feeling.”

“I’d like to go out an take a look at that cave, Captain…You want to go with me?” asked Padrino.

“Yeah, let’s do that. When?”

“How’s tomorrow suit you?”

“I’ll come out there and pick you up about ten.”

"I'll be ready. Bring some smoked ham sandwiches, too," said Padrino.

"Sounds good."

SANTA FE DEPOT
GAINESVILLE
1898

Bone and Mason stood on either side of the metal steps leading up to the second passenger car, allowing the girls to board ahead of them. They had full carpet bags in each hand.

"I'd offer my hand, Pard, but it's kind of full," Bone said as Loraine stepped up on the stair.

"Damn you, Bone, do I look infirmed?"

"Well, not so you'd notice, hon…Just trying to be polite."

"Turning over a complete new leaf, huh, Bone?" said Mason grinning.

Loraine had her shoulder strap purse and wore her dark gray travel trousers and black thigh length cutaway morning coat that covered her Kimber .45 on its gunbelt around her waist.

Fiona was similarly dressed except she wore her pencil-roll brim black gambler's Stetson and with a red paisley bustier under her coat. Her twin .38-40 ivory-gripped Colts in reverse draw, showed as bulges under her coat.

Bone and Mason also had their side arms under their thigh length black frock coats. Bone, his 500, .50 caliber Smith & Wesson and Mason his stag-handled Colt .45, plus a snub-nose .38 long Colt birdshead in a shoulder holster.

Mason turned to Bodie who had walked up to the train, hitching the team out front of the depot that brought them in the carriage.

"Still averaging a train robbery every four days in Texas?" asked Mason.

"Yep, 'cording to the cap'n down in Austin. If any numb nuts try to hit the train, it will either be between Ft. Worth an' Waco or Waco an' Austin… Keep your eyes open," replied Bodie.

"Always do. 'Preciate the ride…See you in about a week or so…Send you a telegram."

"Ya'll have a good time," said Bodie.

"Plan on it." Mason grinned as he followed Bone up the steps.

"All aboard…All aboard for Ft. Worth, Waco, Austin, SanAntone…All aboard," yelled the blue clad conductor as he walked alongside the train on the red brick platform. He waved an *all right* at the engineer leaning out the side window of the cab of the black 4x4x2 coal-fired, steam locomotive.

The big wheels started to slowly rotate as the engine chuffed, breaking the inertia of the seven car passenger train.

The locomotive began to pick up speed as it headed south out of Gainesville. It would be at full speed of fifty miles an hour by the time they passed the small community of Valley View.

"Well, we're under way, kids. Anybody hungry?" asked Bone

"It was almost one o'clock when Faye had lunch, Bone," said Loraine.

"Yeah, sweetheart, but it's almost supper time…somewhere."

"You can wait."

"That's what my mama always said to me," mumbled Bone.

"Are you hungry all the time?" asked Fiona.

He shrugged. "Pretty much…Think I was born that way…always figure I never know when I might get to eat again."

"Actually, love, I could eat, too," added Mason.

"What are we going to do with this pair, Loraine?"

"I don't know," She sighed. "Feed them I suppose."

"Now you're talking," said Bone.

Fiona opened the picnic type wicker basket and handed each of the men a drumstick along with a slice of Faye's fresh bread.

"Yum." Flynn took a big bite. "Oh," he said as he chewed. "Bodie said there's still a train robbery in Texas about every four days an' that if they was to hit us, it would…" He took another bite. "…most likely be between Ft. Worth and Waco or Waco an' Austin."

"Don't talk with your mouth full, dear," instructed Fiona.

"Not…Just swallowed," said Mason.

Fiona and Loraine exchanged glances and they both rolled their eyes.

The train slowed as it rolled into Denton for water and any passengers. The engine stopped just past the water spigot from the tower. The fireman crawled up on top to pull down the filler pipe and release the water into the tank in the tender behind the locomotive that also held the coal bunker. The operation took no more than four minutes.

The conductor waved at the engineer as the last passenger boarded. The big locomotive chugged out of the station and was underway again.

It passed the small town of Sanger without stopping since the flag wasn't up and continued on toward Ft. Worth.

"Well, that hit the spot. May make it to Ft. Worth, now," said Bone as he wiped his mouth with a napkin.

"It's less than an hour, Bone," replied Loraine.

"I know, dear, that's why I said I may make it to Ft. Worth…emphasis on *may*."

She shook her head. "My God."

Loraine and Bone sat on the east side of the car, facing forward. He had the aisle seat. Fiona and Mason were directly across the aisleway, also facing forward with Fiona on the aisle. They sat almost in the center of the semi-crowded passenger car.

Two rough looking men in worn dark broadcloth suits and bandanas over the bottom half of their faces, stepped through the forward door from the first passenger car. They had their guns drawn.

"Now, folks, in case you don't realize why we have our guns out…well, this is a holdup," said the shorter of the two men. He pointed his Colt first at Fiona, and then waved it down the west side of the aisle.

"It would be wise if nobody done nothin' stupid, like tryin' to be a hero. We ain't gonna hurt nobody…"

"Less'n we have to," interrupted the taller man to his left and slightly behind him.

"So, all you fellers git your wallets an' pocket money out an' put it in big boys hat there…'long with yer watches." The first speaker nodded at Bone's dark green John Bull hat.

He pointed his gun at Fiona again. "An' you ladies jest empty yer purses an' put yer rings in there, too…Now, ya'll do it right now an' we'll be on our way."

Bone got to his feet and removed his hat. “This the hat you’re talking about, slick?”

“Huh? Yeah, give it to me an’ sit your big ass back down.”

“No…Don’t think I will,” Bone replied.

“What did you say?”

“I said, I don’t think I will…As a matter of fact, I’m going to break you in several pieces, sunshine…You pointed your popgun there at my great grandmother. That’s a real big no-no and really makes me mad.”

“Huh?…Are you crazy!” The robber backed up a step as Bone moved forward holding his hat out in his left hand.

“I have been accused of that, yes…But, my name is Bone…and I’m your worst nightmare, pal.”

“”The hell you say.” The highway man thumbed back the hammer on his .45, but, before he could pull the trigger, Bone’s massive right hand shot forward like a striking cottonmouth, wrapped around the pistol and the man’s hand, and squeezed.

The outlaw screamed in pain and the scream went up a full octave as Bone wrenched the gun from his hand, breaking his trigger finger in the process in addition to his thumb.

The road agent's partner to his left, swung his Remington to point it at Bone, but froze halfway as the sound of three Colts being cocked and Loraine racking her Kimber occurred simultaneously. Fiona had drawn both her .38-40s.

The color drained from his face as he saw the four deadly weapons being pointed directly at his head.

"My hand! My hand! You broke my hand! the first man screamed.

"That's not all friend. Like I said, I'm your worst nightmare."

Bone dropped the man's gun to the floor and swung his ham-like fist up and down on top of the shorter man's head with a hammer strike. It looked almost like his head was driven down between his shoulders as his eyes rolled up to just show the whites and he collapsed to the aisleway like so much dirty laundry.

"What did you do to my brother?" yelled the taller man as he dropped his own gun to the floor.

"I gave him a free sample...Now turn around and put your hands behind your back." Bone took a set of cuffs from the back of his gunbelt and snapped them on the man's wrists.

"Ow, ow, that's too tight."

"And that's too bad…You fellows picked on the wrong train. My wife and I are police detectives, that gentleman over by the window is a High Sheriff and this lady here…is a Deputy US Marshal."

"Oh, damn." He looked down at his brother. "He gonna be awright?"

"Probably not…I imagine he's going to be a little shorter."

The conductor burst through the forward door and quickly took in the situation. "Oh, thank the Lord. I'll put these fellers in the privy up front till we get to Ft. Worth. He glanced at the badges on their vests and bustiers. Can't tell you how much the railroad appreciate's ya'll…I'll see your complete fares are returned and additional passes issued."

"Much obliged," said Bone as he helped the groggy first man to his feet.

Mason handed him his cuffs. Bone secured the partially out cold man's hands behind his back like his brother's.

The conductor took the two brigands forward to the tiny men’s privy on the right side of the car, crammed them inside and locked the door.

Bone sat back down, glanced at Loraine and then at Fiona and Mason and grinned.

“Well, that was fun, children…Bodie lied.” Bone chuckled. “His captain will have to rework his actuarial tables on train robberies on the Gulf and Colorado.”

Fiona looked across the aisle at Bone and backhanded him across his shoulder. “Great grand mother?…Damn you, Bone.”

He shrugged his big shoulders. “Needed to get his attention.

“You did that when you said, ‘I don’t think so.’,” said Loraine.

§§§

CHAPTER SEVEN

ROSA'S CANTINA
SAN ANTONIO

It was near closing time as Vernon staggered to his feet from the table where he'd been sitting all afternoon, nursing a bottle of mescal. He wobbled toward the back door and stepped out into the dark alleyway.

Vernon glanced around, he could just make out the privy in the starlight, but that wasn't his destination. He shuffled over to some used whiskey barrels just outside the back door that Rosa used to hold trash.

He collapsed to the ground between them and the adobe wall of the cantina and promptly passed out.

Rosa had shooed the rest of the patrons out the door and went around blowing out all the lamps, but one. She took the last of the trash outside to put in the barrels and saw Vernon on the ground, curled up next to the still warm adobe against the night chill.

Knowing she couldn't pick him up, Rosa went back inside, grabbed a blanket, took it back out and covered him. She watched him for a moment, then shook her head, wiped the tears from her eyes and went back inside.

CENTRAL TEXAS

The sun was breaking the eastern horizon as Bone stirred and blinked his eyes. He glanced off to the east over the top of Loraine's head at the first vestige of the golden disk poking up, chasing the night away. Then he looked west as the bucolic Texas countryside flashed past outside.

The morning rays hit the three hundred foot high Balcones Escarpment that separated the Edwards Plateau in the west from the Coastal Plains eight minutes after the sun woke from it's lair. The Balcones Fault underneath the escarpment, extended from the Rio Grande all the way up to the Arbuckles in the Nations.

Bone nudged Loraine. "Hey, Pard, you ever seen the escarpment at sunrise?"

She raised her head up from under his huge arm where it had rested most of the night and looked out the window on the other side of the car. "Um?...Oh, my...it's beautiful, isn't it?"

Their voices woke Fiona from her intermittent slumber on the jostling of the railroad car and the clack-clack of the steel wheels. She glanced over at Bone and Loraine looking across her and Mason, out the window on their side.

"What is it?" she muttered sleepily.

"Look out your window," suggested Bone.

Fiona turned as the morning sun now fully illuminated the escarpment. “My goodness. I never knew that existed…but, then again, I’ve never been to this part of Texas before.”

“Well, I was raised down here, but, I’ve never seen the Balcones at sunrise,” said Loraine.

“It’s such a marked difference from this grassland we’re on now. How far is it over there?” asked Fiona.

“Around twenty miles from the railroad tracks here to those ridges and hills. It’s called the Texas Hill Country…runs from what we’re looking at, northwest up to Llano and west to Luckenbach. Artesian springs, waterfalls, crystal clear rivers and creeks abound…It’s beautiful,” commented Loraine.

By now, Mason was also looking. “I’ve been down here. Hunted over around Llano…Good lookin’ country, all right.”

“Think the train will get to San Antonio on time?” asked Fiona.

“Should,” answered Mason. “Only had about a ten minute delay while the sheriff’s deputies back in Tarrant County were taking those ne’er-do-wells into custody.”

"Got anything left in the basket?" asked Bone.

"Some roast beef sandwiches, chicken neck, gizzards and liver and a pickle," answered Fiona as she peeked under the lid of the basket.

"Love me some livers and gizzards…go great in the sandwich with the roast beef…Be better with some salsa, though," said Bone.

"Oh, yuck, Bone…Fried chicken, roast beef and salsa?"

"Don't know what you're missing, Pard."

"I'll sacrifice that part…if you don't mind."

"You don't like sardines, cheese and crackers, either…and they're staples."

"Lucky me," Loraine replied.

POSSUM KINGDOM LAKE
2018

Captain St. John parked his black squad car between the cliff overlooking the lake and the ridge just to the north with the cave.

"Wear your hiking boots, Padrino?"

"Moccasins…Won't slip on loose rock like shoes or boots."

"Damn, I shoulda thought of that," said St. John. "Even though these combat boots served me pretty well in Afghanistan."

"Uh-huh…They rotted out pretty quick in Nam."

The two former Marines worked their way up the slope to the cave entrance. Padrino held up his hand to stop when they were outside the opening.

"Feel that?" asked Padrino.

"What?"

"We're heavier up here. Can't you tell?"

"Now that you mention it, I do feel just a little sluggish."

"There's more gravity here…Probably even more than if we were at the equator. This is that gravitational anomaly I mentioned."

"And that means what?" asked St. John.

"It creates a unique electromagnetic area that draws lightning during a storm…or possibly even heat lightning during the summer that can form a vortex. I suspect it can even be activated during a perigean super full moon or a blue moon."

"What's a perigean super full moon?"

Padrino chuckled. "It's when a full moon occurs at the extreme of the lunar perigee…when the orbit of our satellite is closest to the earth…It looks about 15 percent larger and around 40 percent brighter. Extra high tides and other things, like a vortex, can occur…Anything that has to do with gravity."

"How do you know this stuff, Padrino?"

"It's a gift."

The older man took out his tac light and stepped inside the mouth of the cave, shining its light around. St. John followed and moved beside him with his light.

"Right," muttered the captain.

"Here's the spiral." Padrino traced the ten inch wide grooved petroglyph with his finger. "Uh-huh, at least fifteen thousand years old. See the slight deterioration of the limestone, even in here out of the weather?…The humidity will have an effect on the edges of the carving over the millennia…Appears to have been carved with a flint point and a rock hammer."

"Well, if they were in here and a lightning bolt hit the cliff…Where the hell did they go?" asked St. John.

"In my opinion, they're still here, Captain…but in a different time."

"When?"

"That is the sixty-four thousand dollar question…When indeed?" said Padrino.

SAN ANTONIO, TEXAS
1898

The Gulf and Colorado pulled into the station, blowing off steam as the engineer brought the big locomotive to a stop alongside the brick depot platform.

The two couples got to their feet. Bone and Mason reached up and pulled their carpet bags from the overhead storage bins.

Bone nodded at the door at the end of the car. "After you, ladies."

"Oh, it's so good to just move around without having to balance, holding on to the seats," said Fiona.

"Like a drunk sailor," commented Bone.

"It's good to move around in any circumstance," added Mason as he opened the door at the end of the aisleway.

The metal door was set across the end of the car with the women's privy between the first seats and the door. The men's toilet was at the opposite end.

It was considered rude to use the facilities when the train was stopped at the station because there were no holding tanks. Bodily excretions went straight to the ground under the car.

Mason went down the four metal steps to the platform, set the bags he had down and held out his hand to assist the ladies.

"Thank you, sir," said Loraine as she twisted her torso back and forth after she stepped away from the railroad car.

Fiona was doing the same. "Oh, that feels so good…Now I know how dogs and cats feel when they stretch after taking a nap."

Bone looked around the platform as the other passengers disembarked and were meeting family or friends or getting transportation. "Wonder where our ride is?"

"Are you looking for transportation to the Villa de la Vega?" asked an attractive woman with a slight Castilian Spanish accent as she walked up.

Mason turned to the raven-haired, fifty plus year

old aristocratic appearing woman with blue eyes and alabaster skin.

"Uh, yes, Ma'am…Are you Sophia de la Vega?"

"I am…My hired help disappeared on me…At least he didn't report for work almost a week ago. He was my gardener and maintenance man, plus he picked up customers in the carriage…I don't know what could have happened to him."

"Sorry to hear…Is your carriage out front?" asked Bone.

"Yes."

"This is Mister and Missus Flynn, Mason and Fiona…And my Par, uh…my wife, Loraine Bone…and folks just call me Bone."

Loraine surreptitiously poked him in the back.

Sophia held out her gloved hand to Mason, palm down. He lifted it gently and brushed her fingers with his lips. "It is indeed a real pleasure, Madam de la Vega."

Bone did the same.

"My maiden name is Rodriguez. I believe Don Flipe Deigo de la Vega was my great…uh, my great grandfather on my mother's side," said Loraine.

"Oh, wonderful, we must talk when we get to the villa," Sophia responded. "The carriage is this way."

ROSA'S CANTINA

"*Señor* Vernon…Wake up…*Señor* Vernon," said Rosa.

He mumbled. "Don't have duty today, Sarg." He rolled over and pulled the blanket over his head.

Rosa picked up an empty whisky bottle and banged on the side of one of the wooden barrels next to his head.

Vernon covered up with both arms. "Injuns!…Git down, git down!"

"Come, *Señor* Vernon, eet's time to get up," she said.

Vernon peeked up as he pulled the blanket down to his chin, momentarily confused. Then his bloodshot eyes squinted as he focused on Rosa.

"Eet's all right, *Señor* Vernon, eet's only Rosa."

"That's a terrible…"

"You can't sleep there, *Señor* Vernon…Eet's morning."

"… thing to do to a man. Especially…"

"*Señor* Vernon, I need to open up to serve breakfast…"

"…somebody who was tortured by the Comanches."

"Comanches?"

Vernon sat up and rubbed his eyes and scraped his tongue across the edge of his front teeth and smacked his lips.

"You were tortured, *Señor*?"

He nodded. "For two days…Was fixin' to hang me upside down over a campfire when my squad rescued me." His eyes jerked around like he was still a little confused.

"I am so sorry, *Señor* Vernon. You come eenside and Rosa will fix you some *huevos rancheros* and *tortillas*…You come. You are safe with Rosa."

§§§

CHAPTER EIGHT

BONE'S RANCH
2018

"Do you have any suggestions, Padrino?" asked Captain St. John as they pulled up in front of the ranch house.

"About getting Bone and Loraine back or finding out when they are?"

"Yes…either or."

"I think getting them back is a nonstarter. I think that if they come back, they'll do it when the gods are smiling…But, I think there is a way to find out *when* they are."

St. John nodded as he killed the engine and glanced over at Padrino. "Well?"

"Let's go inside. Thank goodness for the Internet…and on the eighth day, God created search engines…We're going to do some research."

St. John shrugged his shoulders and opened his door. "I'm with you…This is way out of my pay grade."

Padrino booted up his computer and gave it a few seconds while his satellite receiver modem came on line.

Tyrin curled up under the computer desk next to Padrino's feet.

"Your satellite system even has WiFi, doesn't it?" asked St. John.

"It does."

"What's your pass code? So, I can hook in with my phone."

Padrino smiled. "Lucy2014."

"Oh, that's cool," the captain said as he logged in.

"I didn't see any power lines coming in the house…You got underground all the way out here?"

Padrino grinned. "Not hooked up to Cooke County Electric Co-op at all."

"Well, then how…"

"Lucy left us her portable solar power generator. It's about the size of a deck of cards and is wireless. Their solar collectors and storage batteries have a few thousand years on ours…She converted this whole house, lights, appliances…everything to wireless."

"You're kidding."

Padrino shook his head. "When her ship crashed at Aurora in 1897, all she was able to salvage before the townsfolk arrived was her emergency kit…A metal case similar to a Halliburton. She carried her formfitting gray space suit, the power generator, two weeks of emergency rations, interstellar transmitter, several bars of gold…and a bag of diamonds in it when she wound up here and adopted by Cletus and Mary Lou Wilson. Left it all to Bone, except her suit when she was rescued."

"So, Tesla was right about wireless power?"

"That and quite a number of other things including electromagnetic wave theory."

"Which you think is the secret to time travel?"

"I do...The problem, as I see it, is control...the how and when. According to Tesla, if time travel is actuated, you go to the same place you are."

"I see...Aw, hell, no I don't, but I understand what you're saying."

"H. G. Wells had it right with his novel, *The Time Machine*...Same place, different times...Wells' actual description of his machine was fairly close to that of an electromagnetic wave generator."

"Huh?...Who knew?...So, just what are we going to research?"

Padrino had slipped on his computer glasses and looked over the top of them at St. John. "Bone."

"Do what?"

"We're going to search for Darrell Ulysses Bone and Loraine Rodriguez throughout history."

"So, you're saying we may be here a while?"

Padrino grinned. "Maybe...Maybe not."

VILLA DE LA VEGA
1898

Sophia opened the thick carved mahogany door, hung by iron strap hinges, of the villa for the group. “I’ll show you to your rooms and let you all get settled in.

“That will be fine, Miz Vega,” said Bone.

“Please call me Sophia.”

“Sophia, it is then.”

“Did you have breakfast on the train?”

“We had a little something we brought. That train didn’t have a dining car,” replied Fiona.

“Well, I’ll fix up a little brunch then, as soon as you come back down.”

“Be fine…uh, Sophia,” added Mason.

Thirty minutes later, the four came back down the stairway and turned into the spacious dining room.

There were four bowls set on the table along with a side plate of some sliced sausages and glasses of iced tea.

"That looks scrumptious," said Fiona as she took a seat at the table. "What's it called?"

"It's called gazpacho, Fiona," replied Loraine. "It's a traditional Spanish cold soup made with fresh vegetables."

"That's correct, Loraine," commented Sophia. "The sliced sausage on the side plate is chorizo, a fermented, cured, smoked pork sausage…also a traditional Spanish dish, and, of course, the Mexican staple of corn tortillas to use to dip into the gazpacho."

"I think I could get used to this," said Bone as he took a spoonfull of the gazpacho followed by a bite from a rolled up buttered tortilla.

"Loraine, you mentioned that Don Felipe Diego de la Vega was your great grandfather, then your great grandmother was his first wife…she died of cholera in '60. Her name was Mamie. The Don and I married in '65."

"One of the things my mother didn't know was where Don Felipe Diego de la Vega was buried," commented Loraine.

Sophia looked down at her glass of tea, and then looked up at Loraine. "Don Felipe Diego de la Vega was a hard, abusive man." She looked out the window into the large atrium in the center of the hacienda for a moment. "I had him buried out back, behind the hacienda by the arbor."

"I understood he died of old age," commented Loraine.

Again, Sophia stared out the window and without turning back, said, "He was hung for beating a child to death with his cane on the street for begging him for money."

Loraine gasped. "My grandmother apparently didn't know."

"How horrible," said Fiona.

"Hanging was too good for him," added Bone.

"I agree…I didn't erect a headstone. He was a hateful, evil man and I'm glad they hung him…Killing that child was the last straw."

Mason looked at her. "He abused you, then?"

She nodded and pursed her lips together.

"What about the suicides?" asked Bone.

Sophia took a deep breath. "He put a curse on the judge who passed the sentence on him, all his relatives and descendants."

"Then you're saying that all the suicides have been relatives of the Judge?" asked Mason.

"What about the one last week…Clayton Armstrong?" inquired Fiona.

"Apparently he was too. According to his widow, Anita, her husband was a third cousin…I didn't know that when they booked their reservations."

"Whoa, that's reaching out a ways," said Bone.

"What was the judge's name?" asked Loraine.

"Judge Barton James McLain," Sophia replied.

"Uh-oh," responded Mason. "My mother's maiden name was McLain."

"You don't think…"

"She never mentioned much about her family, so I don't know," said Mason.

BONE'S RANCH
2018

"We're going to focus on north Texas, since according to Tesla and others, like I said, if they were transported from that cave…they came out in that cave."

"What time period are you going to search?" asked St. John.

"Going to start with the last two hundred years."

"Why two hundred?"

"Gut feeling. If there's nothing there, we'll widen the search…If I know Bone, and he's back in time, history will most likely mention him."

The captain shook his head. "You and Bone…Every time he's working on a case, he says, 'Always follow your gut'."

Padrino grinned. "Right more often than wrong." He keyed in *Darrell Ulysses Bone*.

A page appeared on the monitor.

"Hmm, hate it when this happens. It's like trying to find a book on Amazon. Shows you everything but what you asked for…'Bone - …rigid body tissue consisting of cells embedded'…"

"Well, duh," commented St. John looking at the screen.

"*Bone - The Complete Cartoon Epic…*" read Padrino.

"That sounds close." St. John grinned.

"Does, but it's modern."

Padrino punched in *Detective Bone*."

The screen showed books and TV shows with the word *Bone* or *Bones* in the titles. Padrino scrolled to the next page.

“Wait, what’s that?” asked St. John.

“Huh…Say’s ‘Assistant Secretary of the Navy, Theodore Roosevelt, helped to foil his own kidnapping by Spanish operatives while on a hunting trip in the Kiamichi Wilderness in the southeastern corner of the Choctaw Nation. He assisted the legendary Deputy US Marshal Bass Reeves, Deputy US Marshal Fiona Miller Flynn, the only female marshal in the Nations, in addition to Deputy US Marshals Selden Lindsey, Jack McGann, Brushy Bill Roberts, and Sheriff Mason Flynn of Jack County. Also assisting in the disruption of the dastardly plan were a Detective Bone and Inspector Loraine Rodriguez of Cooke County, Texas’…”

“Holy Mother of God!” exclaimed St. John as he sat down heavily in a chair. “When is that?”

“November, 1898,” answered Padrino.

“Well, you might know Bone and Loraine were going to get involved in something…Anything else?”

Padrino chuckled. “Here’s more…’Sheriff’s deputies D.U. Bone and Loraine Rodriguez of Jack County, instrumental in solving a string of killings of law officers in a four county area of north Texas,

Jack County, Clay County, Wise County and Montague County'…" He looked over at St. John. "Mid November, 1898."

"There's got to be more," said St. John.

"Uh-huh…and 'Sheriff's deputies of Jack County foil stagecoach robbery in northern Jack County when four road agents tried to holdup the Henrietta to Jacksboro stage. Deputy Bone was asked who the brigands were. He replied, "Don't know, don't care…they shot my partner…they didn't survive to be interrogated." Deputy Loraine Rodriguez is back in Jacksboro recuperating.' I'll be darned," said Padrino.

"Anything else on Loraine?"

"Nope, nothing."

"Well, I'd say that pretty well narrows it down, don't you?"

Padrino nodded and then got a huge grin on his face. "You are not going to believe this one."

St. John leaned over to see the monitor…

§§§

CHAPTER NINE

ROSA'S CANTINA

"What has happened to you *Señor* Vernon? You have been in my cantina before, but only drank coffee with your meal," commented Rosa as she set a plate of *huevos rancheros* and *tortillas* in front of him.

Vernon played with his food for a moment, and then looked up at Rosa. "One of our guests, Mister Armstrong, hung himself last week."

Rosa put her hand to her chest and then made the sign of the cross. "Sweet Mary."

"I'm the one that found him hangin' there…Seen too much killin' an' death in the Injun wars in Arizona an' north Texas…Jest couldn't handle it, Miz Rosa…Jest couldn't handle it."

"You poor man, I weel say the rosary for you…I have a bed in the storage room in the back. You will stay here until Rosa can feex you. You see."

VILLA DE LA VEGA

"I understand you told Ranger Hickman you felt something wasn't right, Sophia," said Bone. "Can you give us some information that might help us? I think the ranger told you that we were all law officers."

Sophia nodded. "*Si, Señor* Bone." She glanced at Loraine and the others. "*Señor* Armstrong was very happy that morning. He and Vernon played chess and drank tea out in the garden, and then he said he was going up to his room to take a nap until his wife, Anita, returned from shopping."

"Did he win or lose the chess matches?" asked Loraine.

"Oh, no, *Señor* Armstrong won all four games. He was a master, you see. He apologized to Vernon for not telling him before."

"And that's when he went up to his room?" inquired Fiona.

"*Si, Señora*."

"What happened then?" asked Mason.

"I took their tea glasses and Vernon and I went to the kitchen where I washed them, and then stirred the marinara sauce I had on the stove. Vernon got a chicken leg from the ice box and I told him not to ruin his supper. He smelled of the sauce…" She smiled slightly. "…and said there wasn't much chance of that."

"What happened next, Sophia?" inquired Bone.

"The signal bell from his room rang, but stuck in the sideways position and I had asked Vernon to fix it and he said he put a brand new rope inside the velvet sleeve, so, I sent him up to see what the problem was."

"He knocked on the door, I imagine," said Loraine.

"*Si*…I could hear him knocking and calling for Mister Armstrong from downstairs and I went up…The door was locked from the inside and I told Vernon to push the key out with his screwdriver and use his master key."

"He opened the door, and then…" asked Mason.

She nodded and wiped her nose with her handkerchief. "Vernon opened the door a little and looked inside. He cried out and fell to his knees…I peeked over him into the room and saw poor Mister Armstrong hanging from the bell pull rope…He was dead."

"Were there any signs of him struggling?" Bone looked at Sophia.

"Oh, no, no…His hands were bound in front of him and his feet were tied together…both with drapery sashes…The stool from the piano in the room was beside his feet…It just didn't seem right."

"I agree, Sophia. I see several things right off." Bone glanced at Loraine, she nodded. "You said his hands were tied in front of him. Two, his feet were tied, and three, the stool wasn't turned over…Correct?"

"*Si...si.*"

"Three or four legged stool?" asked Loraine.

"Three…Oh, what a terrible tragedy. He was such a nice man. I really don't understand…"

Loraine interrupted her, "Yes, Ma'am. But, I just would like to get your observations on his demeanor…"

"I do not understand word, 'demeanor'."

"His state of mind, his mood, when he and his wife…"

Oh, *si, si.* Very outgoing, happy. Love to talk. He love to play chess with my hired man, Vernon, They played all afternoon…I just don't understand why Vernon up and quit the very next day…"

"Yes, ma'am. Uh…He quit the next day?" Bone interrupted.

"*Si.* Actually he just never came back…even to collect his pay."

"Really? That's interesting," commented Fiona. "Did you notice if he and Clayton had any arguments or disagreements at all that afternoon?"

"No, no, *Sigñora*, they were very, how you say…congenial, that is except when Vernon 'checked' Mister Armstrong and the very next move, Mister Armstrong 'checkmated' Vernon…But, they then just laughed it off."

"And Vernon didn't leave the kitchen until you both heard the bell from Armstrong's room?" asked Mason.

"No, not at all."

"Which room were the Armstrongs in?" asked Bone.

She looked at Fiona and Mason. "Yours."

BONE'S RANCH
2018

"I don't believe it!" exclaimed St. John. "Bone and Loraine married!"

"What the article from the Gainesville Daily Register, November 28, 1898, says…'Ceremony performed at Skeans Boarding House on Lindsey Street by Doctor Winchester Ashalatubbi from Ardmore in the Chickasaw Nation. The bride was given away by the legendary Deputy US Marshal Bass Reeves'…"

"Lord, Lord…The US Marshals Service still considers Reeves as the greatest marshal in their history…Served over 3,000 felony warrants…and never failed to execute one he was assigned. One bad dude and one hellova lawman…Even arrested his own son once." St. John chuckled. "One time, he had paper on one Myra Maybelle Shirley Reed Starr…Better known in history as Belle Starr. She turned herself in to Marshal Bud Ledbetter in Muscogee, when she found out Reeves had paper on her…saying she didn't want Bass Reeves on her tail."

"That's funny…Read about him. Lot of folks think he was the inspiration for the fictional character of the Lone Ranger." Padrino grinned. "You know, the Lone Ranger always gave out silver bullets to citizens that helped him and Tonto and Bass Reeves gave out…silver dollars."

"Didn't know that, now," said St. John. "But, you might know that Bone and Loraine would get to know him…and to have Bass Reeves to give her away…Wow! That means they are…or would you say, were, pretty close."

"Either or both…Yeah, even I didn't see that coming. Their relationship has always been like oil and water…Kind of remind me of Tracy and

Hepburn in *Adam's Rib*...Apparently she finally knocked his wall down."

"What about her wall? I always felt she just tolerated him and his antics."

"Good question," said Padrino.

"Who else was at the wedding?" asked St. John.

"Well, Sheriff Mason Flynn of Jack County was his Best Man and, get this, her Matron of Honor was Deputy US Marshal Fiona Miller Flynn...Cooke County Sheriff Walt Durbin was there, and so was Texas Ranger Bodie Hickman."

"Damn, would have loved to been there."

VILLA DE LA VEGA
1898

"Are you concerned that you are in the same room?" Sophia asked Mason and Fiona.

They exchanged looks.

"I don't think so. Give us a good chance to go over the room carefully, looking for any possible clues that your local people might have missed," said Fiona.

"Oh, the local deputies didn't look for anything. They just assumed it was a suicide and left it at that."

"Not surprised," commented Bone.

"What can you tell us about the other suicides?" inquired Mason.

"Well, they began about six months after Don Felipe Diego De La Vega was hung. I had started taking in boarders and visitors to San Antonio shortly afterward…Since the hacienda is so large."

"And you think each one was related to the judge in some way?" asked Loraine.

"*Si*, it was several years before I noticed the connection."

"Was there anything else special you noticed?" asked Fiona.

Sophia glanced at her and Mason and finally nodded. "Interestingly enough, they all hung themselves…and all in the same room…Yours."

"Oh, my," said Fiona.

"Could we see the burial site?" asked Loraine.

"Of course, follow me." Sophia led the way out into the atrium garden and out the back gate.

"Over there by the arbor." She pointed.

"That dead area?" asked Mason.

"*Si*, nothin' will grow on it. I have planted, fertilized with chicken manure, watered over and over…"

"Is there rock underneath?" inquired Bone.

Fear started to show in her eyes. "No, we buried him very deep and put a concrete slab over the coffin, and then filled it back in."

"Why a concrete slab?" asked Loraine.

She glanced around fearfully again. "Because, as I said, he was an evil, evil man, *Señora*…Plus I had the local priest do an exorcism over the site."

"You feared him that much?" Fiona looked in her eyes.

"*Si, Señora*. I think he was possessed by a demon…possibly Satan himself…And still, nothing will even germinate there, not even weeds…I finally put a bird bath on it…and…and the birds won't drink from it or even bathe in it…I think the very ground is cursed."

"Anything else, anything at all you can think of?" asked Bone.

"Well, I have had some of Don Felipe Diego De La Vega's relatives stay here on occasion and they've sworn to me they've seen him roaming the halls."

"Only his relatives?" asked Fiona.

"*Si*…The local priest feels that only the descendants of Don Felipe Diego De La Vega, can see the spirit that roams the hacienda…He performed an exorcism on it last year…" Sophia looked at Loraine with a slight degree of pity. "You are the first relative that has stayed here since…I would understand if you wanted to stay elsewhere."

Bone and Loraine exchanged glances…

§§§

CHAPTER TEN

VILLA DE LA VEGA

The four law officers sat around the parlor, drinking iced tea.

"Well, before we get started on the cop stuff…don't think it's going anywhere…what say we take a stroll and see some of the sights?" said Bone.

"Excellent idea, Bone," replied Mason.

"I agree," concurred Fiona. "That's why we came, after all."

Loraine nodded. "Even though the suicides and the possible ghost story are fascinating…they'll keep."

"Should we ask Sophia for some suggestions?" asked Fiona.

"Let's just wander and see what comes up. I know we're not far from the Alamo and the *mercado*," said Loraine.

Bone got to his feet from the embroidered settee. "Lead on, then, o great Spanish conquistador."

"Damn you, Bone, don't get in trouble now," Loraine said as she backhanded him across the chest.

He worked his eyebrows up and down, twice. "Just figured we were on a conquest, since you speak the native's lingo."

Loraine rolled her eyes. "Come on…Get thee behind me, Satan."

"Ooh, good one, Pard."

"Can't wait to see what kind of trouble you're going to get us into," she added.

"Yeah, me too," Bone responded and swatted Loraine's butt playfully.

"Not time to get romantic, Bone."

"Oh, darn."

"I thought ya'll would quit sniping at each other after you got married," said Mason.

Bone cocked his head at him. "What's the fun in that…grampa."

"Damn you, Bone, don't you start with that," said Fiona.

He giggled as he followed Loraine out the door.

They walked downhill through the sylvan area that bordered the San Antonio River on both sides and crossed the narrow bridge that had been replaced numerous times due to flooding. The river started with springs close to present downtown San Antonio, and then joined the Guadalupe River.

"What say we stop in that cantina there and get a beer, or better yet, see if they got some of that Cactus Wine before we go on down to the Alamo?" suggested Bone.

"Now you're talkin'," agreed Mason.

Bone pushed the batwing doors open for the ladies and they entered the darkened Rosa's

Cantina. They walked up to the bar after their eyes adjusted to the semi darkness.

"Good, not too crowded," said Loraine. "And smells about like the saloons back in Jacksboro except for the pepper ristras hanging about the room."

"What'd you expect, Pard?" asked Bone.

"It appears we're a little ahead of the rush," commented Fiona.

A clean cut, fifty year old, wiry, leather-faced bartender walked up and noticed their badges.

"Good afternoon, officers, what'll ya'll have? My name's Vernon."

"You got any Cactus Wine?" asked Bone.

Vernon cocked his head and arched an eyebrow. "Well…yes, sir. Have you ever had Cactus Wine before?"

"Once," replied Bone.

"And you want it again?"

"Sure…But, only one." He held up one finger.

"Ah, you have had it before." Vernon grinned.

"You could say that," said Loraine glancing at Bone.

Vernon set four gill shot glasses on the bar, turned around, took a wicker covered bottle from the counter behind him and filled them with the pale amber liquid.

"I would just sip it if I were you…don't want to slam it back."

Bone nodded and grinned. "Been there, done that."

They picked up the four ounce glasses, clinked them and each took a slight sip.

"Um, that is smooth," said Fiona looking at Vernon.

He nodded and smiled. "Uh-huh…and that's the danger…uh, Marshal."

"I can testify to that." Bone looked back to the bartender. "You said your name was Vernon?"

He wiped a nonexistent stain from the polished bartop. "Yessir, Vernon Wyland."

"You look like cavalry," said Mason.

"Yessir, was…twenty-five years."

Mason nodded. "I remember you trooper. I'm Captain Mason Flynn…You were in my company up north when we were chasing the Comanch."

"Yessir, recognize you now."

He paused. "You got captured, didn't you?"

Vernon paled, stared down at the bartop and nodded. “Quanah Parker’s Kwahadi bunch caught me.”

“I sent a squad in to rescue you…They stampeded their horses and when the warriors ran to catch them, they came in, cut you loose from that stake and got you out of their village.”

“Yessir, I wouldn’t be here if they hadn’t. The Kwahadi medicine man, Isa-tai, was makin’ a example of me for their people.” Vernon took a deep breath. “Seein’ how much torture I could stand before I died…He gelded me, an’ then was skinnin’ the hide from my back…in little strips.” He looked away and bit his lower lip. His entire body quivered with emotion.

Loraine took a sharp intake of air. “I am so sorry, Vernon…You worked over at the Villa de la Vega for Sophia, didn’t you?”

Vernon’s eyes widened. “Yes, ma’am. Gardener and maintenance man…till last week…That’s when…when I found Mister Armstrong.” His eyes started to fill up. “Just hangin’ there.”

“Do you mind if we ask you some questions…The Texas Rangers asked if we would investigate this incident while we were here…Things just don't seem to add up."

He nodded.

"What kind of mood was he in that afternoon, Vern?" asked Bone.

He took another breath. "Pretty damn…sorry ladies…good, you ask me. Beat me like a redheaded stepchild…That's why I couldn't never understand why he…Uh…" Vernon pursed his lips and looked down again.

Loraine gave him a few seconds to gather himself. "I have a couple of questions for you Vernon…One, did you have an argument with Clayton Armstrong while ya'll were playing chess?"

His head jerked up and he almost shouted. "I didn't have nothin' to do with him killin' his self!…"

Bone interrupted him. "Vern, we're just trying to get to the bottom of this thing…Something's not addin' up…Like we mentioned. Now, did you have an argument with him?"

"I wouldn't call it a argument…Finally checked him after three games an' he immediately checkmated me…beatin' me four straight…couldn't win for losin'."

Sophia told us you never came back for your pay…What's that about?" asked Loraine.

"Well, uh…when I saw him hangin' there, in his room…dead…Kinda lost it, you know? Couldn't understand it neither…His hands was tied, but I could see from the door his fingers was bloody around the nails, you know?…Seen too much dyin'…Friends an' settlers shot, burnt, hung, or all cut up an' scalped in the Injun wars…even little kids. I kinda uh…fell back into the bottle…" He looked up again. "You know?"

"How come you to start workin' here?" asked Mason.

"Miz Rosa, she found me out in the alley passed out next to her trash barrels an' made me come inside. She cleaned me up, fed me, gave me a place to stay back in her storeroom and gave me this job of work to do…Guess you could say she saved me…I owe her. Tell Miz de la Vega I'm powerful sorry, but I just couldn't go back in there."

"She said you mentioned something about 'ghosts' when you looked into the room," said Fiona.

Vernon nodded. "I know I seen Mister Don Felipe Diego de la Vega in the room. They's a big painting of him in that room…That's how I know who it was."

"You mean you saw a person?" asked Bone.

"Yessir…Only thing is…he wasn't all there."

"What do you mean, Vernon?" questioned Loraine.

"I could see plumb through him…It was like he was underwater, but I could see the bed on the other side of him…You know?"

Mason and Fiona exchanged glances.

"We saw the painting," said Fiona.

"You're stayin' in that room?" asked Vernon.

Fiona and Mason both nodded.

Vernon made the Catholic sign of the cross.

BONE'S RANCH
2018

"Well, any ideas?" St. John asked Padrino.

"Not really, except maybe keep trying to get through on his phone again…I think it's obvious there's a gravity anomaly zone around the police station."

"I've been doing it three or four times a day since he disappeared...Peach told me that it was still on, somewhere...That was the first time I got through to anything but the answering system...You think there's anywhere else there could be one, beside the cave and the station?"

"No tellin'...There could even be a zone here on the ranch...There is equipment that can measure the gravitational pull of any given area, but I sure don't have one and have no idea where to get one, besides maybe NASA...."

"Joy."

"You try every time you think about it...and so will I. Don't know what we'd do if we did get him, but, I'd like to try,' said Padrino.

ROSA'S CANTINA
1898

Vernon stepped down the bar to wait on some Mexican vaqueros. One of the men had a long drooping mustache and silver conchos down the side of his black leather pants. He also wore a matching bolero jacket and a silver embroidered black sombrero hung down his back by a braided *barbiquejo*, turned and looked down at the Americans.

"Hey, *gringos*, whatchu do with a pretty *señorita*?…She's too good forchu, *gran hombre*."

Bone looked at the vaquero, noticed his black silver concho and stud decorated gunbelt. It was strapped low around his hips with a mother-of-pearl handled Colt Peacemaker in cross-draw on his left side.

"You got a problem, Pedro?" asked Bone. "And, by the way…it's *señora*."

"Oh, no, *gringo*. He paused, got a puzzled expression on his face, and looked at Bone. "How chu know my name es Pedro?"

Bone grinned. "If I told you, I'd have to kill you."

The Mexican laughed, showing his single gold front tooth and punched his friend next to him. "Oh, *gringo*, chu *cómico*, you no keel Pedro….Pedro Ruiz keel chu and take the *señora*, no?"

Bone laughed out loud and stepped down the bar to Pedro. The Mexican gunhawk drew his Colt, but before he could thumb back the hammer, Bone's hand shot out like a striking rattler and snatched the pistol away. He held the gun up and looked at it closely.

"Got a new shooter, I see, Pedro." Bone glared at him. "And the answer is…no." He simultaneously drew his .50 cal from under his coat and shoved it under Pedro's chin, lifting him up on his toes.

Bone thumbed back the hammer of the huge handgun, leaned down and whispered in Pedro's ear. The swarthy-skinned gunslick turned pale as his eyes got big and the whites showed completely around them. A yellow puddle gathered about the sole of one of his black, silver toe-capped, knee-high boots.

A malevolent laugh rumbled softly from deep in Bone's throat.

"*Sí, sí, Pedro va*," he croaked. "*Pedro va*."

Bone let him down.

"¿Puedo tener mi arma…mi pistola," asked the gunhawk meekly, pointing at the Colt.

Bone just stared down at him stoically.

He repeated, "*Sí, sí, Pedro va*." He turned and quickly headed to the doors and outside.

His friends looked up at Bone and started backing away, completely out the batwings after Pedro.

Bone giggled and headed back to Loraine, Fiona and Mason.

"What the hell was that about?" asked Mason.

"Remember me telling ya'll when we were up in the Kiamichis with Teddy Roosevelt about the Mexican gunhawk that Bass and I convinced to leave?"

"Oh, you used Lucy's bracelet to make yourself invisible, said you were the Spirit of the Seven Devils and kept his gun and gunbelt," answered Loraine. "And that he and everyone with him would die," commented Loraine.

"He left the country and was supposed to head back to Mexico," said Fiona.

"What did you tell him when you whispered in his ear? He got pale as a ghost." asked Mason.

He giggled again. "Told him I was the messenger from the Spirit of the Seven Devils sent to see if he went back to his country…Told him he didn't go far enough and the Spirit was angry…very angry."

Loraine laughed and hit Bone across the chest. "You are so bad, you big lug."

He grinned. "I know."

"I love you."

"I love you too, Pretty."

He picked her up off the floor by her waist and they kissed.

§§§

CHAPTER ELEVEN

BONE'S RANCH
2018

"You know, Captain, I think I do have something I want to try," said Padrino.

He walked over to his bookcase and took out a leather covered jewel case from a shelf and opened it.

"Well?"

Padrino held up a six inch long, forest green, translucent, teardrop-shaped crystal.

"Is that an emerald!" asked an incredulous St. John.

"Nope it's a tectite type of crystal formed from the impact of a giant meteorite…Called a *moldivite.* It was given to me years ago when I was a young man by an old Navajo Shaman when I studied with him…He said it amplifies, channels and expands the energy of certain people's spirit energy…The Shaman indicated that I was one of these people. It's not the same as a natural quartz with standard six-sided crystals that are uniform and they grow that way…no forming crystal within the 'mother' crystal of *moldvite* is repeated like a natural crystal because it doesn't grow…it was formed on impact…Each and every one of the molecules are different, like snowflakes, because part of it is terrestrial and part is extraterrestrial…That make sense? "

St. John held out his hand. "No…May I?"

Padrino handed thc stone to him. "Light…and warm." He looked up at his friend. "Is it vibrating?"

Padrino nodded.

"Wonder where it came from?"

"Most likely from the meteorite crater area near Flagstaff, Arizona. The Shaman said he'd had it for years, it was given to him by his mentor, who had also had it for years…It's known as the Canyon Diablo Crater that was formed some 50,000 years ago in the Pleistocene epoch when a fifty meter wide meteorite impacted the area…This is a very large, museum quality *moldivite* crystal.

"So, what do you intend to do with it?" asked St. John.

Padrino's light brown, gold-flecked eyes twinkled. "I'm going to the cave where we know there's a very strong gravitational anomaly, plus there's a full moon this evening which will increase its strength."

"And?"

"And I'm going inside with the crystal and enter into a state of zen meditation and see if it's enough, with the crystal's help, to activate the electromagnetic vortex and transport me back in time. The world of quantum physics has proved that thoughts are responsible for controlling and directing energy."

St. John stepped back and sat down heavily in his chair. "Are you nuts?"

"I'm a Marine."

St. John nodded. "'Nuff said…Don't know why I asked, Master Guns, my brother…What do you want me to do?"

"Take me there…If it works, don't want my truck to be found abandoned like Bone's Thing."

"Good thought. When?"

"What time is it?"

An hour later, St. John's vehicle stopped back at the cliff near the cave.

Padrino got out, grabbed his rucksack from the back seat and slipped it over his shoulders. He checked his .45 caliber 1911A Colt that he had carried in 'Nam'.

"Got plenty ammo?" asked St. John.

"No such thing, Captain, you know that."

"Right. Got an extra box in my trunk if you want it."

Padrino looked askance at him.

"Right." St. John popped the trunk of his car and took the box of .45 ACP Colt rounds out and slipped it into Padrino's ruck when he turned around.

"Well, got a canteen of water, couple of MREs, three pounds of jerky, some smoked ham, couple of loaves of my bread, my fishin' kit, matches, flint, my K-Bar, money, and phone…Think I'm good to go."

"What kind of money? They won't recognize our paper money."

"Gold and silver coins."

"What'd you pay for the silver?"

"Average of about eighteen dollars."

"Eighteen dollars that will be a dollar in 1898?"

Padrino nodded. "Know how much a dollar would buy in 1898?"

"Oh, right…good idea, but, why your phone?"

"Worked for you and Bone…might work for me under the right circumstances, plus it has a recorder and a camera."

"Another good thought…How are you going to find him and Loraine if this works?"

"Go to where we know they're deputy sheriffs…Jacksboro. It's about twenty-five miles north from here and that's just…"

St. John grinned. "'A little stretch of the legs, right?', the Duke's line from *The Quiet Man*."

"Yep, one of my favorite movies…He should have won the Oscar for that one," said Padrino.

"Agreed…What if you don't go to the right time?"

"Then I'll try to get back," answered Padrino.

"'Do or do not. There is no try.'…"

"Master Yoda."

St. John nodded and tilted his head up at the cave. "Shall we…I'm going to watch."

"You might get sucked in by the vortex."

"Just a minute…I'll get another box of ammo."

VILLA DE LA VEGA
1898

The four sat around Fiona and Mason's room after unloading the trinkets, clothing and carvings they had bought at the *mercado*.

Bone set the bottle of Cactus Wine he bought on the dresser. "Boy, don't know about ya'll, but I got chill bumps walking around the Alamo."

"Me too," said Loraine. "Talk about spirits…I could feel them all around there."

"You too?" asked Fiona.

"Spooky," added Bone as he handed the CSI kit to Loraine. "Well, shall we get started?"

"What do you expect to find? It's been over a week."

"Edmond Locard's theory of exchange principle states that, 'Every contact between two items, leaves a trace. It cannot be wholly absent. Only human failure to find it, study and understand it, can diminish its value.'," said Loraine.

Excuse me? Who the hell is Edmond Locard?" asked Mason.

"Director of the very first crime lab in existence…It was in France," answered Fiona.

Bone started tapping the walls, while Loraine took scraping samples from the bell pull into a bindle.

Loraine looked over at Mason. "Pull the drapes for a moment, please…I want to check for blood,"

"What?…How?" he asked.

"I'll show you."

He pulled the thick, heavy drapes, shutting out the light coming from outside.

Loraine took out her bottle of homemade Luminol.

"What's that, Loraine?" asked Fiona.

"It's called Luminol in our time. I made some up with an alkaline solution of hydrogen peroxide. Blood will glow blue for a few seconds in the dark."

She put a small amount in her mouth, and then blew it out in a fine mist like the Cowboy running back, Zeke Elliott, does with water before a game, on the crushed area of the dark green velvet where Clayton Armstrong's neck would have been.

"Nothing…He did not tear his nails from clawing at the rope," she said.

"His hands were tied anyway," said Bone. "But he could have possibly reached up with both hands, I suppose."

Fiona dusted for prints on the three-legged piano stool with the ground graphite powder. She examined it with a strong magnifying glass.

Mason checked the window. "Hasn't been opened in years."

"I don't find any prints on the piano stool, Bone, even on the underside," said Fiona.

"I did find some epithelials where the ropc was tied around his neck, and a mixture of some at arm level, where guests pull the rope, but, none on the end. I don't see how he could have possibly tied the knot," stated Loraine.

Well, kiddies, I found the ubiquitous secret passage, I think," said Bone.

"Say what?" commented Loraine as she stopped her examination of the pull rope.

"Mason, come over here and help me move this armoire."

"I thought secret passages were only in the movies," said Loraine.

"The what?...Oh, right, I remember, the play acting thing on moving pictures," commented Fiona."

"Right...They are used a lot in horror or scary movies," replied Loraine. "Great great grandfather de la Vega was anti-slavery...This house may have been part of the underground railroad for escaped Texas slaves," added Loraine.

Bone and Mason grabbed the heavy armoire and pulled it out.

Bone tapped on the panel behind it. He pushed on it and it sprung open to reveal a narrow passageway leading to a stairway down.

"Maybe the killer came and went this way," said Fiona.

Bone shined his light inside. "Uh-uh…Don't think so…There must be a quarter inch of dust on the floor…Not disturbed. There hasn't been anybody in here for over fifty years."

THE CAVE
2018

Padrino and St. John stepped inside and shined their lights around.

"Hasn't been anybody here but us chickens," said St. John.

"Would appear so."

Padrino moved to the center of the cave and took the crystal from the large side pocket of his old time olive drab BDUs. He sat down in the sand in the lotus position and snugged his Marine Corps Veteran ball cap down on his head.

"What do you have to do?" asked St. John.

"I'm going to hold the crystal in both hands, and then I have to clear my mind and start my meditation."

"That's it?"

"Well, not quite. Look outside and see if that full moon is rising. It's a few months from perigee, so that will help…not quite as much as if it were a blue moon, but maybe close enough."

"Blue moon? Isn't that when there's two full moons in the same month?"

"It is, but there won't be one of those until June 18 of this year…seven months from now. We have 'em every two to three years," said Padrino.

St. John walked to the front of the cave, which faced east and looked out at the moon. It was about halfway up the horizon and appeared huge and yellow.

"Be up in about five minutes," he commented as he moved back to the area in front of Padrino.

"Well, I can get started then. Takes me about that long or longer to get into a zen state and if this is going to work…it'll be then."

"I don't know how you do it. I can't ever seem to clear my mind…too much going on at the station."

"That's really one of the prime reasons to practice it…to still the mind."

"Easy for you to say."

"One of the advantages of being retired." Padrino smiled, shook his head and took several long clearing breaths, relaxed, and then closed his eyes.

"You don't have to do this."

"I think I already have," commented Padrino.

St. John glanced back over his shoulder at the moon still rising. In just a few moments it would be in perfect alignment with the cave opening and would fill the cave with its pale yellow moonlight.

Padrino was still as a statue in his lotus position. His breathing was almost nonexistent.

The moon had cleared the horizon and it's light now flooded the inside of the cave. St. John glanced back to look and marvel at the giant orb that seemed to cover the entire entrance of the cave a moment and when he turned back to Padrino—he was gone…

§§§

CHAPTER TWELVE

VILLA DE LA VEGA
1898

Bone, Loraine, Sophia, Fiona and Mason are seated around the dining table, finishing off the last of the Spanish lasagna.

"Sophia, I don't know when I've had better lasagna," said Loraine.

"I'll A-men that," added Mason.

"What makes this so different from Italian lasagna?" asked Fiona.

Sophia smiled. "Well, I use fresh chorizo sausage, casings removed, my own recipe of marinara sauce, chopped fresh cilantro, chopped green chiles, ricotta cheese, freshly whipped cream, two large lightly beaten eggs, and my own lasagna noodles."

"Well." Bone chuckled. "You made enough for an army…or me."

Sophia smiled bashfully. "I don't like anyone to leave my table hungry."

"I notice there isn't any left…" Loraine looked at Bone. "What'd you have, honey…three helpings?"

"Waste not, want not…" He grinned his enigmatic smile. "You weren't bashful either…My *acushla*."

Loraine kicked Bone under the table.

Sophia smiled. "That's Gaelic."

Bone nodded. "Yessum."

She got to her feet, stepped over to the mahogany buffet at the side of the room and poured four snifters of brandy.

Sophia set the crystal, short-stemmed glass snifter in front of each. “Veccio 800, ‘76…That’s 1776.”

Bone nodded as he too a sip. “Quite liberating…My, my, this is a first class facility.”

“That’s a terrible pun, Bone,” said Loraine.

“I know…Couldn’t help myself.”

“You never can,” she replied.

“I’m impulse control challenged.”

“Well, this brandy will make you sleep like a baby.”

“Will it stop someone from snoring?”

Bone shot Loraine a look. “Me?…Or yourself, Pard?”

She kicked him again.

Mason held up his snifter. “To good food and good company.”

They all nodded and took a sip.

Bone shook his head. “Like drinking silk.”

Fiona finished off her brandy and set the snifter on the table.

“Well, I hate to break up such a rousing party, but, it’s been a long day…We must have walked five miles today,” said Mason.

"Didn't you say your mother's maiden name was McLain, Mason?" asked Sophia.

"Yes, Ma'am." Her family was from south Texas."

"I hope ya'll are not too superstitious about staying in that room," said Sophia.

"No, Ma'am, doesn't bother me much," answered Mason. "You, hon?"

Fiona shook her head. "Not really."

"Mason doesn't believe in superstition…he thinks it's bad luck," quipped Bone.

"Bone!" snapped Loraine.

He shrugged his shoulders.

"Another example of his impulse control being challenged," said Fiona as she got to her feet. "Well…night all. Coming, love?" She smiled seductively.

"Right behind you, Pretty."

"Good night, Mason…Fiona…sleep well," commented Sophia.

"Don't let the bed bugs bite."

"Bone!" Loraine kicked him again under the table.

THE CAVE

Padrino blinked his eyes and took several deep breaths and looked around in the dark cave. “Captain! Captain St. John!”

There was no reply. He rose slowly to his feet, assisted by his right hand, thinking, *Wow, getting down here was easy, but getting up is something else altogether...Getting old definitely ain’t for sissies*.

He walked slowly to the front of the cave. The full sphere of the moon was well above the entrance.

Padrino glanced down the slope of the ridge toward the cliff’s edge where St. John’s car was parked. It was gone—so was Possum Kingdom Lake.

“I’ll be damned,” he muttered. He put the crystal back in his right side pocket. “Just as well spend the night in the cave and reconnoiter in the morning…Definitely not in 2018…but I wonder when I am.”

He moved down the hill, scouting for firewood.

Twenty minutes later he headed back up to the cave with an armload of deadfall. He dropped it just inside the entrance against the north side wall and started breaking small twigs from some of the wood into tiny pieces.

He stripped some of the loose bark from a piece of long dead cedar and rubbed the brown fibrous material between his palms, turning it into a reddish powder.

Padrino scooped a hole in the sand at the front edge of the cave near the pile of wood on the north wall and laid a larger piece of the cedar bark in the middle. He dumped the powder in the center and began to build a teepee over the top of it with the small, broken twigs, and then added larger pieces.

Padrino took a match out of his waterproof tin, struck it on limestone rock next to the hole he had dug and held it against the cedar punk he had put underneath the teepee. Smoke began to curl up through the twigs and then a yellow flame flared and licked the underneath side of the twigs.

In a short moment, they caught and soon thereafter, the larger pieces began to burn.

"Well, haven't forgotten how," he muttered.

He got his small coffee pot and a plastic bag of ground French Roast coffee out. After pouring some water from his canteen, he dropped a large handful of the coffee in the pot, put the lid back on and set it on the rock close to the fire.

Padrino then took a bone bun out of his ruck and the bag of his smoked ham. He sliced the bun in half with his K-Bar and laid a bunch of the ham in between.

"That ought to do it."

He looked toward the entrance on the other side of the fire and saw two red glowing eyes above the ground just outside.

Padrino pursed his lips and chirruped several times. The sound was repeated from outside and the glowing eyes came closer. He chirruped again, and again was answered by a large raccoon standing on its back legs and walking to the edge of the cave.

"Hungry, girl?" asked Padrino.

The raccoon chittered back.

The wily Marine vet took a chunk of ham from the bag and pitched it at the feet of the big sow. She dropped down to all fours, picked up the meat with her remarkable human-like front paws.

The raccoon held the meat with one hand and brushed the sand from it with her other, and then peeled a bite from the chunk with her teeth.

Then she turned around and gave a piece to each of the two kits behind her, and then ate the rest herself.

The female raccoon looked at Padrino and chittered again.

He tore a large piece from the bone bread bun and pitched it to her. This time, she caught it in the air, tore several pieces of the chewy bread off and gave it to her family.

Without fear, after they had eaten, she led her two offspring inside and over to the opposite wall behind a couple of rocks where there was a pile of grasses.

"Huh…Looks like I've usurped your den, m'lady." Padrino grinned at her. "Hope you don't mind me sharing."

The raccoon sow chittered back at him, turned around several times like a dog and laid down in a curl with her babies snuggled against her stomach for the night.

"I'll be gone in the morning, madam, not to fear."

Padrino smiled again, checked the coffee and found it was ready. He took a metal granitewear cup from his bag, filled it and stepped outside the opening.

He stood, mesmerized at the beauty of the skies overhead, blew across the top, and then took a sip.

"Oh, my, my…Nothing like this in my time."

The moon was almost directly overhead and, though full, was not as bright as when it was just rising. He looked off to the north and easily found the North Star and the Big Dipper.

"Amazing, just amazing…Completely unspoiled by the light pollution of modern times, it's as though…"

He was interrupted by a large, very bright shooting star or meteor arching across the black blanket of the star strewn night from southwest to northeast. "Star light, star bright…The first star I see tonight…I wish I may…I wish I might, Have the wish I wish tonight…"

Padrino finished the ancient nursery rhyme, sotto voce, then his lips pursed and a single tear rolled down his weathered cheek.

WILSON/BONE RANCH
1898

Lucy sat bolt upright in her feather bed on the north side of the Wilson's house and rushed to the window in time to see a large meteor streaking across the night sky.

She got a puzzled look on her pixie face, slowly walked back to her bed, crawled in and pulled her covers up to her chin. Lucy stared at the beaded ceiling, lit only by the moonlight streaming in her window, for a long while and finally drifted back off to sleep. She mumbled a word she'd heard only in Bone's mind, "Padrino?"

VILLA DE LA VEGA
1898

"I think I'm about ready for bed also," said Loraine.

"Thought you'd never bring it up." Bone looked over at Sophia and grinned. "Our wedding night, you know."

Loraine blushed.

Upstairs, Loraine stepped out of the attached dressing room in a long white cotton granny gown.

"Did you wear your armor under that?"

"You'll have to find out on your own, big boy." she replied with a grin.

"I sleep commando."

"Not here, you don't, mister, you're wearing PJs or I'll shoot you…You can wait till we get back to Jacksboro to go commando…No telling what's going to happen tonight."

"Killjoy…But you do have a point."

"I know," Loraine replied grinning again and winking at him.

Moonlight streamed in through the window later that night. Bone sat up, threw back the covers and stood on the floor, wearing only his red long john bottoms.

He then started walking slowly toward the wall where a shadowbox holding an antique Spanish Vaquero's fifty foot braided rawhide riata was mounted. He opened it, took out the riata and walked to the large vertical mirror on the wall.

Loraine's eyes snapped open when Bone opened the shadowbox.

Bone reached up to the top of the mirror and pushed a hidden catch. The mirror swung open and revealed an opening in the wall. He stepped in, extended his hand upward, pushed another hidden catch, and then eased the opposite mirror in Mason and Fiona's room open.

Bone stepped through into the semi-dark room, lit only by the moon light coming in between the partially closed drapes on the window.

Loraine quickly got to her feet wearing only her long white granny grown and followed him through the opening. She stepped into the room just behind Bone.

She watched him open the riata, take the honda loop in his right hand and walk to the Flynn's bed.

He stood next to the bed and dropped the honda loop over the top rail of their four poster, pulled it down and draped the noose over Mason's head…

§§§

CHAPTER THIRTEEN

THE CAVE
1898

Padrino continued to stare in awe at the black blanket of diamonds with an amazingly crystal clear full moon directly overhead. He took another drink of coffee and stopped in mid-sip. “Lucy?”

He sat down in the sand in front of the cave, put his coffee cup aside and once again went into his zen mode.

For the next five minutes, he and Lucy communicated. It can't really be called a conversation as much as a linkage or exchange of information and images. He knew her thoughts, memories and feelings and she knew his.

Even though they wouldn't originally meet until 2014, Lucy knew of their relationship from Bone's memories—again the paradox of the folds in the time and space continuum.

He knew she was at the very ranch in the same room where he and Captain St. John were that morning, searching for information on Bone, but, 120 years in the past.

Padrino picked up his cold coffee cup, pitched the remaining coffee and the grounds to the dirt and got to his feet. He looked up at the sky once again before turning and heading back into the cave.

He refilled his cup with hot coffee and stepped back to the front to take a sip and look back up once more. "See you soon, Lucy…my sky queen," he muttered.

VILLA DE LA VEGA
1898

Bone underhanded a few coils of the riata over the four-poster rail above Mason's head. He dropped the rest to the floor and started to take up the slack.

Loraine moved quickly behind him. She grabbed the side of his thick neck and pressed on a certain spot in his nerve center at the base of his skull using her many years of study in the martial arts.

Bone released the rope and collapsed to the floor like a side of beef beside the riata coils.

A gaseous apparition emitted from his body. It turned and looked directly at Loraine. It appeared exactly like the life-sized portrait of Don Felipe Diego de la Vega downstairs. The apparition then walked straight to the wall and disappeared into it.

Mason awoke with a start and grabbed the rope about his neck like it was a snake and slung it to the side.

"Son of a bitch!"

He saw Loraine standing beside the bed and Bone on the floor in the pale moonlight.

"What are you doing in our room?…How did you get in here?"

He reached over and turned the wick up on the coal oil lamp beside the bed, partially illuminating the room as Bone got shakily to his feet. Loraine grabbed his arm to steady him.

"What are you doing, Pard?"

Loraine quickly released it.

Mason and Fiona were both sitting up in the bed.

"Again, what are ya'll doing in our room?"

"Your room?…How did I get…" Bone looked around, confused.

"Let's get some clothes on, go downstairs and make some coffee…Not sure ya'll are going to believe this," said Loraine.

An hour later, the four were in the kitchen, they had been joined by Sophia, who heard the racket of Bone stoking up the fire in the cast iron wood burning stove.

She held the coffee pot and offered a refill to everyone as they sat around the kitchen table.

"So you're saying that the ghost of Don Felipe Diego de la Vega was responsible for those suicides? And you saw him?"

"I don't know what I saw, Sophia." Loraine rolled her cup between her hands, staring at it.

"*Señora*, didn't you mention that priest said only descendants of Don Felipe Diego de la Vega, would be able to see the spirit that roams the house?"

"*Si*, and several have, as I mentioned."

Loraine stared at the surface of the dark liquid in her cup for a long moment before she spoke, "*Señora* de la Vega…I know you had the spot where you buried him exorcised…and it hasn't seemed to help…but as his next of kin…I feel it only proper to rebury him in consecrated ground…Maybe then he'll be at peace."

She nodded. "I will contact the priest in the morning."

**SAN FERNANDO MISSION CEMETERY
SAN ANTONIO, TEXAS**

A middle-aged Catholic priest sprinkled holy water over an ornate casket and blessed it. Four altar boys stood by the grave site flanking the priest. One held a large crucifix, another the heavy church bible, the third held the holy water, and the last, the incense.

Bone, Loraine, Fiona, Mason, Sophia, and even Vernon, stood by, observing.

Loraine laid a white carnation on the casket and made the sign of the cross.

VILLA DE LA VEGA

The four sat around the kitchen once again. They were joined by Vernon from the services. Sophia served midday sandwiches.

"So, we still don't know if those people actually committed suicide or not," said Mason.

"Just instinct," replied Bone.

"I found no definitive evidence...one way or another," added Fiona.

"Maybe ghosts don't leave a trace," said Loraine.

Vernon got to his feet.

"Where you going, Vern?" asked Bone.

"Down to St. Mary's...Think I need to light some candles...This is way too spooky for me."

Upstairs in Mason and Fiona's room, the image of Don Felipe Diego de la Vega reclined in the four poster canopy bed. He twirled a white carnation back and forth between his thumb and index finger.

JACK COUNTY, TEXAS

Padrino trudged along a rutted, dusty, ranch road, really not much more than a cattle trail, to the north, headed, not to Jacksboro, but to the Wilson Ranch where Lucy was.

He knew from connecting with Lucy, that Bone and Loraine weren't at Jacksboro, but were on their honeymoon in San Antonio.

He shook his head and grinned for the umpteenth time. "Could of knocked me over with a feather…Who would have thought…Love it."

Padrino approached a clear, limestone bottomed branch that crossed the trail. He unslung his canteen, shook it, and then knelt down beside the small stream and marveled at the water.

"Huh…clear as a bell. Not like in my time." He

cupped his hand, dipped up a palm full and drank. “Mmm, sweet. Like my well water.”

He poured the small amount of tepid water remaining in his canteen after making coffee last night and this morning on the ground and held the aluminum container under the water until it filled. After screwing the cap back on, he slung it over his shoulder, got to his feet and continued on north.

Padrino looked up ahead to see two scruffy cowboys trotting their ponies along the trail, heading in his direction. He stopped and leaned against a large post oak that grew next to the trail and pulled out a piece of peppered jerky to chew on.

The two men reined to a stop in front of him.

“Mornin’, pilgrim, them’s some funny lookin’ clothes yer a wearin’,” said the younger of the two.

“Depends on who’s looking at them.”

“Huh…Headin’ to Jacksboro?” the older nearest one asked.

“Not so’s you’d noticc. Going morc toward Rosston.”

“Got a bit of a hike, there, then, I’d say, old man,” said the other, a younger, a rather smarmy individual.

“Not bad. Rather have a horse, though.”

“You got enough money to buy one, old timer?” asked the first man.

“Probably,” replied Padrino as he tore a strip of the tough meat off and chewed it.

“What say you give us the money an’ we’ll go git you a horse an’ bring it back?”

“How do I know you’ll come back?”

“Why, don’t we look honest?” The smarmy one looked at his brother.

Padrino grinned. “Do you really want me to answer that?”

“You sayin’ we’re liars?” the older man raised up in his saddle.

“Didn’t say that.”

“Well, what er you sayin’?” asked smarmy.

“Just asked if you thought you looked honest.”

The older man looked at the other and grinned. “Don’t know ‘bout my little brother here, but I damn shore do…Now how ‘bout it?” He spat a long stream of tobacco down near Padrino’s boot.

“I don’t think so.”

“Then how ‘bout you jest give us that pack you’re a carryin’. That where yer money is?” the younger brother asked.

"I guess not."

"Well, 'pears to me you ain't got much of a cherce there, old timer. It's two against one…Now shuck it." The older brother drew his battered Colt and pointed it at Padrino.

"Yeah, 'fore I step down an' stomp a mudhole in yer skinny old ass," said smarmy.

Padrino chuckled. "Well, you boys are making a big mistake…But you see, that's the point, I'm too damn old to take an ass whipping…so I'll just have to kill you."

He shucked the ruck from his right shoulder and swung it off with his left hand, drawing his .45 clipped to his belt in the back under his Carhartt Duck Chore jacket in the process. It was pointed at the nearest man when his rucksack hit the ground.

The man's focus was on the odd looking bag when it fell as was his little brother's. When they looked up, Padrino's semiautomatic was pointed at the older brother.

"What the hell?"

"Is that a gun?" asked the younger brother.

"It is. It's a .45 caliber, seven shot semiautomatic."

"Haw, looks like a toy!" said the younger one as he drew his Remington six gun.

At the same time, his brother thumbed the hammer back on his Colt.

The silence of the bucolic woodside was shattered by what sounded like one explosion. Both of the road agents flipped backward out of their saddles, hitting the ground with dual thuds almost simultaneously, sending up a joint dust cloud.

Padrino shook his head and grinned as he walked toward the two horses that had spooked a little at the gunfire, but stopped about fifty feet away and were nibbling on winter grass at the edge of the road. "Time and effort will take care of ignorance…but stupid is forever," he muttered in wonder at the two cretins lying in the road behind him.

Padrino picked up the reins of the best looking of the two horses, a blue roan gelding, stepped up in the saddle, grabbed the reins to the other, a blood bay gelding and walked them back to where the two highway men and his ruck lay.

He got off the horse, bent over to check on the two men. The older brother was dead, but the younger was straining for his final breath. His mouth was working, but no words came forth, only frothy blood.

He had hit both a little left of dead center of their chests.

"Tried to tell you boys…Never mess with an old Marine…he'll just kill you."

The smarmy man sighed out his death rattle. The heel of his left boot drummed a tattoo on the hard, packed dirt of the road for a couple of seconds as he died.

Padrino tied his ruck behind the six inch cantle on the roan with the long saddle strings. He stuck their gunbelts and guns in the saddlebags after removing them and going through the men's pockets. There was a total of fourteen dollars and twenty-two cents that he transferred to his own. "Spoils of the battle."

Padrino stuck his foot in the stirrup, dallied the lead he'd tied to the other horse's bridle around his saddle horn and trotted off down the road to the north.

"Well, son, you're not the best looking cayuse I've ever seen, but you sure beat walking."

§§§

CHAPTER FOURTEEN

GULF & COLORADO RR

The two couples sat in much the same position in the passenger car of the northbound, coal-fired, train as they had when they rode it south.

“If this trip to San Antonio is representative of what a honeymoon is like…think I’ve had enough,” said Mason as he stared out at the countyside flashing past at fifty miles an hour.

"Don't let your alligator mouth overload your jaybird rear, mister," replied Fiona.

He turned back to face his wife. "Well, you know what I mean, sweetie."

"No, what do you mean…sweetie?" she responded with a coquettish grin.

"Well, I…uh…"

"Best way to get out of a hole, Sheriff, is to stop diggin'," offered Bone from across the aisleway.

"Actually, I thought it was great fun," said Loraine. "We got to relax and enjoy one another, shop, see things we haven't seen before, eat great food, scare the pee out of a gunhawk…and solve a mystery."

"And play a little grab ass."

Loraine kicked him. "Damn you, Bone."

He got a huge grin on his face. "Ow…Well, it's the truth, *Acushla*."

Loraine grinned and replied, "I know, but did you have to let the whole world know?" She glanced around to see how many of the other passengers in the car were snickering.

"Yeah, easy for you to say, you didn't have a rope around your neck…Did we really solve it?" asked Mason.

"Close enough," replied Bone.

"Who's going to believe it…ghosts an' all?" Mason looked at the big man.

"Oh, probably the same people that believe in aliens and time travel…to start with," Bone said with a mischievous grin.

"Well, I thought it was fun, too," added Fiona.

Bone turned to Loraine. "You know, Pard, I've been thinking a lot about my Padrino."

"Gettin' homesick?" she asked.

"Actually…Not really. I grew up wanting to live back in the old west, but I do miss my Padrino."

"Now, who is Padrino again? I know you've mentioned him before," asked Mason.

"My mother's cousin and my Godfather…he's a Shaman…Spirit teacher…We're descended from the Nasca in Peru…Him and me, on my mother's, mother's side. He basically raised me…My folks were killed in an automobile crash when I was twelve."

"Oh, I'm so sorry, Bone. He must have been a wonderful man," said Fiona.

Bone chuckled. "Still is. He's only seventy and tough as ten year old rawhide...Retired Marine Corps Master Gunnery Sergeant...fought in a war we had or will have in our time in Viet Nam...a jungle conflict."

"How many wars does our country have in the future?" asked Mason.

"Too many," offered Loraine. "Let's see, the next one coming up soon is the Spanish American War, that's going to be a quickie, then there comes World War I...That starts in 1914 and goes for four years..."

"She's only naming the big ones. There were a whole raft of little conflicts in between the biggies," interrupted Bone.

Loraine continued, "Then World War II...it lasted six years. Next was the Korean War...three years..."

"Then the Cold War with Russia...not much fighting, just a lot of sabre-rattling and threats of nuclear war till about 1988..."

"What's a nuclear war?" asked Fiona.

"That's another story all together...let's just say we invented a weapon that could destroy the world several times over and both sides had it...The US was the first to get it and we used it to end WWII…"

"Oh, my," said Fiona.

"And that was a good thing," Loraine interrupted Bone. "With both sides having it, now, each knows that fighting with them could end life on this planet as we know it…"

"It was like they're afraid of us and we're glad of it," added Bone.

"And pretty much from the '60s on, there's been constant conflict in southeast Asia or the Middle East," continued Loraine.

"That's pretty much a continuance of the age-old battle between the Christians and Muslims…Like the Crusades…Throw the Jews in there, too…I was in that one in Afghanistan," added Bone. "Now you see why I've always wanted to live back in this time?"

"I think so…The more things change, the more they stay the same," said Fiona.

"Pretty much," replied Bone.

"That was somethin' that has always amazed me."

"What's that, dear," asked Fiona.

"How you can hate someone and go to war with them just because they don't believe the way you do...One believes in God and the other, Allah...I don't understand," answered Mason.

Fiona grinned. "You're not alone, but if the truth were known...they're one in the same."

"How so?" asked Mason.

"The Jews and Christians worship the God of Abraham or *Abram*, as he was known and so do the Muslims."

"I'm assuming you're going to tell us how that worked," questioned Bone.

"Well, you see, *Abram's* wife *Sarah* was barren and couldn't have children, so she gave him her maid servant, *Hagar. Hagar* bore *Abram, Ishmael*...Then, thirteen years later, God made *Sarah* fertile and she bore *Abram,* a second son, *Issac...Ishmael's* half brother."

"Okay?" Bone had a puzzled look on his face.

Fiona smiled. "*Issac* became the father of Judaism, and of course, Christianity...*Ishmael* is considered the father of Islam...So, both worship the same God...*Yahweh* and *Allah*...is the God of Abraham."

"And they want to fight and kill each other over semantics," stated Loraine, shaking her head in wonder.

Mason added, "But, we have our problems, too…The Indian wars, remaining outlaws…"

"Ya'll remember *Anompoli Lawa* telling us the name of the Amerindian's…or at least the Muskogean language speaking tribes of the southeast…God or the Great Spirit is called, *Chí-hóo-wah*…"

Fiona interrupted Bone. "Which sounds like *Jehovah*, one of the Hebrew names for God in the *Torah*."

"Too close for comfort…Regardless of what he's called…I think you're right, we all worship the same god…" said Loraine.

"Yeah, I agree, Pard…but, this *is* a whole lot simpler time," interrupted Bone. "Now, unless there's going to be a quiz on religion…back to my Padrino…One of the things he taught me that has served me well, especially bein' a cop, was to look at nothing, but see everything…Which was the same identical thing Lucy said to me…or will say to me."

"He sounds very interesting," said Fiona.

"Oh, he is. Lucy really thought so…they would talk for hours…Just the two of them."

"Well, I for one, will actually be anxious to get back to work bein' a Sheriff…Hope Gomer hasn't had any problems," commented Mason.

JACKSBORO, TEXAS
1898

Gomer sat at the desk in the sheriff's office, going through a new stack of wanted dodgers. Newton got to his feet from beside his place by the stove and growled at the door.

"What is it, boy, we got company?"

The thick paneled wood door swung open and two hardcase appearing men stepped inside. Both were dressed in dusty, dark, three piece suits and they needed a shave. Each wore dirty gray Stetsons and had pistols strapped low around their hips.

"What can I do for you fellows?" asked Gomer.

"Where's Sheriff Flynn?"

"Uh, he's outta town on his delayed honeymoon. Anything I can do? I'm deputy Gomer Platt."

"When's he due back?"

"Tomorrow, sometime, he said."

Both men drew their sidearms and pointed them at Gomer.

"Get on your feet and shuck that iron on your side, boy," said one of the men.

"Huh?"

"Now, Deputy Platt!...Not in the habit of repeatin' myself."

Gomer unbuckled his belt and laid it with his Colt on the desk and backed away.

The hair on Newton's back rose up as he growled at the two men from deep back in his throat.

"Better corral that mutt, Deputy, 'fore I plug 'im...Don't like dogs anyhoo."

"Newton, hush...Lay down."

The Border Collie grumbled, stepped back to the stove and lay down, his brown eyes still on the two.

"Just who are you fellows, anyway?" asked Gomer.

"Well, not that it's gonna make any difference...We're the Rudabaugh brothers. He's Frank an' I'm Harlan."

"Rudabaughs...You Henry's..."

"Yeah, Henry was our baby brother and Flynn kilt him or was responsible for it…We aim to return the favor," said Frank.

"Just the two of you? Against the sheriff and his wife, Deputy US Marshal Fiona Miller Flynn?…This oughta be interestin'."

The brothers looked at each other and laughed. "For yer information, boy, we got ten men already scattered about your little town here…Got you shut down an' locked up tighter'n a jug whilst you were in here playin' with yer papers," said Harlan.

"Nobody leaves an' anybody comin' in stays or dies…How you like them apples?" commented Frank.

"What about the town marshal?"

Frank chuckled. "As a lawman, he's useless as tits on a boar hog. Didn't take him three seconds to see the light an' pitch in with us."

"Seems he don't like the sheriff much, neither," said Harlan.

"Where'd ya'll come from? Ain't never heard 'bout you 'round here."

"Arizona is our normal stompin' grounds, Deputy. Only heard about his posse killin' our baby brother last year, a little over a month ago…Took us a while roundin' up our boys and head thisaway," said Frank.

"We spent a month gittin' a mad on, comin' here, an' ain't 'bout to be trifled with. We're gonna hang Mason Flynn...an' probably his wife too, 'fore we leave," added Harlan.

"Yeah, but, just so ya'll know, it wasn't Sheriff Flynn's posse...it was a vigilante bunch...Headed up by the brother of the banker the gang kilt durin' a robbery," commented Gomer.

"What was *his* name?" asked Frank.

"Hiram Merkins...but don't matter none, he got bit in the face by a rattlesnake and died at the same time yore brother got shot."

"Then who was it that shot him?" inquired Harlan.

"Uh, well, that don't matter none neither, he don't work here no more."

"I asked who the hell was it what shot him? Dammit!" shouted Harlan shoving his gun under Gomer's chin and lifting him up on his toes.

"Uh...it was a posseman named Slim Parker."

"An' just where the hell is this posseman?" asked an increasingly agitated Frank.

"Uh, he works out at a horse ranch southeast of here, the Flyin' L.…He's a Chickasaw Freedman."

"A nigger? A smoke kilt our brother?" Harlan screamed. "Sonofabitch! Then he dies, too…Dammit to hell!"

"Naw, Harlan, let's don't hang 'im," said Frank.

Harlan turned to his brother. "What'n hell do you mean, Frank?"

"Let's burn 'im."

§§§

CHAPTER FIFTEEN

GAINESVILLE PD

"He just disappeared?" asked an incredulous Inspector Stella Johnson.

Captain St. John nodded. "I turned around to check on the moon rising and when I turned back…he just wasn't there anymore. Could easily see his imprint in the sand where he was sittin'…but he was just plain gone."

"Ooh, this is gettin' creepy…Oh, what about Tyrin?"

"Somebody's going to have to go out there and take care of him."

"I'll go…Actually, Peach and I will just move out there till Padrino and Bone get back…We share an apartment anyway. Can't leave Tyrin out there alone."

"Good thinking…What if they, uh…don't come back?" asked St. John.

"Well, we'll just stay out there. My gut tells me they will be back, though…sometime."

"Also, how about the three of us keep callin' both of them…Hell, the three of them with Loraine."

Stella giggled. "Still can't believe they're married…What if it's one of Bone's gags?"

"You can pull the newspaper article from the Gainesville Daily Register, November, 28, 1898, about their wedding up on the net and read it for yourself."

She shook her head and her long blond tresses, tied back in a low ponytail, swung back and forth.

"I told Peach, I thought they were in love…but, didn't know it or weren't willin' to admit it…but, you could see the chemistry a mile off." Stella giggled again. "Do you know if Padrino went to the same time period?"

"Don't have a clue, but maybe we'll get through eventually on the phone to one of them," said St. John.

"And maybe Lucy will pop in soon in one of her holograms like she has before."

St. John looked at her. "Yeah, maybe."

JACK COUNTY

Padrino pulled rein at a southeast to northwest wagon road. "Bet a nickel this is the Jacksboro to Fort Worth road." He chuckled. "Be interesting if the folks today knew this would be called the Highway to Hell in the '50s, with all the gambling halls and bars that will be built…What say we swing by and pick up some supplies, and maybe get some lunch, horse?"

The blue roan turned his head and looked back at Padrino with his limpid brown eyes.

"Thought you'd agree. It's only a couple of miles out of the way to Rosston."

He squeezed the gelding up into a road trot to the northwest, the blood bay gelding tracking behind on his lead.

Padrino came into sight of Jacksboro a couple of miles up the road and noticed the crumbling remains, off to the west of the road a little, of what was once the largest military installation in the nation with 666 officers and enlisted personnel during the Indian wars. It had been abandoned in 1878.

"Pity," muttered Padrino. "Glad the Texas Parks and Wildlife Department took it over in 1968, salvaged many of the buildings, and turned it into a state park."

He saw what appeared to be travelers camped in the ruins with three wagons parked nearby. "Hmm, that's interesting. Wonder why they don't go on into town?…Let's go see, shall we, boy?"

Padrino reined to his left and trotted into the former parade grounds. Several children that had been playing in the open, disappeared.

Three men stepped out of the shadows of one of the dilapidated barracks, each held a Winchester, pointed in his direction.

He held up his right hand. “Hold on there, boys, no call for guns. I’m just passin’ through.”

“Step down off’n that hoss, mister, an’ keep your hands where we kin see ‘em,” said one of the men, bringing the rifle to his shoulder.

“You shore are dressed funny,” said the man.

“I’m…uh, from up north. Toward Chicago way.”

“Yankee,” said the second man.

“What’s this about?” asked Padrino as he dismounted.

“You with that bunch in town?” the same man asked.

“What bunch?”

The three men exchanged glances.

“There’s a gang what’s taken over the town…Nobody can leave an’ ‘nybody what goes in…stays.”

“You mean they’re holding the town hostage?” asked Padrino.

“That’s the long an’ the short of it…Takin’ yer life in yer hands, goin’ in there.”

“My boy an’ his boy…” The man nodded at the other farmer type next to him. “…went in this mornin’ to git some supplies…bacon an’ flour an’ sech, fer us. We’re headin’ to New Mexico…They ain’t come out.”

The second man spoke up. “Some youngsters snuck out from the side of town an’ slipped into this here abandoned fort. Tol’ us what it was that was goin’ on…They’s afraid to go back in.”

“What about the law?”

“Said the sheriff’s outta town…They’s only one deputy an’ they got him locked up in his own jail…Them outlaws, bunch of real hardcases, is wantin’ to kill the sheriff when he gits back,” said the first man.

“You don’t say?”

“Yep, what the youngsters said.”

“Wonder when the sheriff is due back? Any idea?” asked Padrino.

“Them boys said he’s expected tomorra…meby the next day,” said the second man.

“Well, I think I’ll just keep on travelin’. Don’t cotton to any trouble,” commented Padrino.

“Sorry if’n we was a mite testy.”

"It's all right. I fully understand…Don't blame you a bit."

He remounted and turned the roan back to the northeast and trotted off. *Need to get to Lucy's by tonight, Bone and them don't need to be riding into that situation, unawares,* he thought as he crossed the road that led into town. *Can switch off on these mounts and should make it by tonight. Probably about thirty miles…as the crow flies.*

CENTRAL TEXAS

The Gulf and Colorado train was slowing down for its scheduled stop in Waco. The locomotive blew off steam as she eased to a stop at the depot for passengers, coal and water.

"What say we get out and stretch our legs while we're stopped?" mentioned Mason.

"Works for me…Maybe we can get some sandwiches," said Bone as he got to his feet and held out his hand to Loraine. "You coming, Pard?"

"I certainly am," she replied as she stepped out to the aisleway.

"I'll go in and send a telegram to Bodie, tellin' him what time the train is supposed to get in," said Mason.

"I'll go with you, dear," commented Fiona.

The four stepped down the steel steps to the platform and headed toward the depot. They passed an apparent law officer with a rough-looking man in front of him in shackles.

"Looks like someone is heading north for a trial," commented Fiona.

"Or a hangin'," added Mason.

"I wouldn't trust that guy a far as I could throw him," said Loraine. "If it were me, I'd have him in ankle shackles, too."

"Agreed," responded Mason.

Bone nodded at the man wearing a deputy sheriff's badge. "Officer."

The deputy nodded back. The prisoner wheeled around when his captor turned to nod at Bone and whipped his shackled hands over the deputy's head, jerking the chain between the cuffs against his throat.

"Everbody back, or he dies."

He pulled back on the chain, lifting the deputy back on his heels, grabbing at the prisoner's hands.

It was obvious the chain had his windpipe shut off as his struggles weakened and his eyes began to bug out.

Bone shot his massive hand out, slamming it down on the top of the prisoner's head, flattening his already battered fedora and began to squeeze.

Almost instantly the man's pull against the deputy's throat lessened as he cried out, "Ahhh."

Bone towered over the pair as he exerted more pressure with his fingers on both sides of the prisoner's head. "Turn him loose or I'll pop your noggin' like a grape…Do it…Do it now," he calmly said.

The man's knees buckled as his eyes rolled back in his head. The deputy was able to grab the prisoner's hands and lift them back over his head.

Bone continued his crushing grip and simultaneously pushing the outlaw down to his knees until he finally went limp and collapsed like a wet newspaper, out cold.

The deputy looked up at Bone in awe. "Ain't never in all my borned days seen anythin' like that," he muttered. "Much obliged, mister."

He finally noticed the badges the four were wearing. "Dangnation, shore glad ya'll was on that train. Thought I was a goner fer shore…That man's a killer. Kilt a whole family in cold blood up in Ardmore. Man and his wife an' seven kids…He escaped durin' the sentencin'. The Rangers caught him over to Gatesville…I'm takin' him back to hang."

"Who was the original arresting officer up in Ardmore?" asked Mason.

"Deputy US Marshal Jack McGann."

They all laughed.

The deputy looked puzzled.

"It's a wonder he survived to make it to trial. Jack doesn't put up with any guff," said Fiona.

"Ya'll know him?" the deputy asked.

They all exchanged glances and grins.

"We do…We do indeed," said Mason.

"Your prisoner's lucky Bone here didn't kill him. He doesn't tolerated 'guff' either," said Loraine.

"Say, who are ya'll, anyhoo?"

"I'm Sheriff Mason Flynn from Jack County, this is my wife, Deputy US Marshal Fiona Miller Flynn." He nodded at Loraine and Bone. "That's Inspector Loraine Bone and man mountain there is her husband, Detective Darrell Bone…We've been on our honeymoons."

"Lord a mercy…Heard 'bout ya'll from Marshals McGann and Lindsey…Lord, Lord, Lord." He continue to look in awe. "Ya'll headin' north, are ye?"

"Gainesville," replied Fiona.

"Shore 'nuff glad to hear that. Sheriff Colcord shoulda sent at least two of us to git this killer."

"Always a good idea," said Mason.

"I'd put ankle shackles on him and shackle his hands behind him, not in front," said Fiona.

"Good idea, Marshal…Uh, what happens if he has to drain his lizzard?"

"Use your imagination," said Bone.

"Oh…right," answered the deputy as he helped the groggy man to his feet and shoved him toward the car. "Thanks again…Move along, jackanape."

Bone jerked like a rabbit had run across his grave. "Padrino?"

§§§

CHAPTER SIXTEEN

COOKE COUNTY
WILSON RANCH

The sun had just ducked behind the horizon and gloaming was in full effect when Padrino rode up to the entrance to the ranch. The first stars were just beginning to twinkle into view to the east in the darkening skies of the coming nightfall.

He could see the white, L-shaped ranch house a little over three hundred yards in the distance. Smoke was curling up from the native rock kitchen chimney and also from the one in the parlor.

"Doesn't look much different, except for the drill stem pipe front entrance and gate Bone and I put in and the galvanized roof instead of our new green one." He nudged the blood bay through the cedar post entry, with the iron Box W brand hanging from the center of the crosspiece, and toward the house. The blue roan on the lead, trotted behind them.

Five minutes later he reined up outside the white picket fence. He recognized a young Lucy with her familiar pixie hairstyle sitting on the porch steps, apparently waiting on him.

She got to her feet and ran to the spring-loaded front gate with Garin right beside her and came outside to greet him.

"Welcome, Padrino." Lucy had a big grin on her cherubic face.

He stepped down from the gelding and wrapped his reins around the hitching rail, leaned over and hugged the diminutive alien.

Padrino stepped back. "Sure am glad to see you, *Annuna*…or I guess I should say, Lucy."

"And I, you…for the first time…You got here sooner than I expected."

He nodded. "Had two horses, I…uh, acquired south of Jacksboro. A couple of brigands decided they didn't need them anymore…at least not where they went."

She smiled again. "I know. I kept tabs on you during your trip. I can't tell you how surprised I was when I sensed you last night…Of course I only know of you and your image from Bone's memories of our time in your yearly count of 2014 when you and he helped me get rescued by my people."

Padrino looked down at Garin. "Great guns, he looks almost exactly like my…or your Tyrin you left with us in my time."

She grinned. "Yes, I love his color of blond and white. That's why I will adopt Tyrin from Noah's Ark Rescue in 2010, according to Bone…because he looked so much like Garin here."

Padrino knelt and rubbed Garin's ears. "I'm still having a little trouble getting my head around all of this, especially how Bone and Loraine came to this particular time…and then I did."

"I know, my Chickasaw Shaman friend, *Anompoli Lawa*, explained it…actually much better than I could."

"Oh?"

"He said it was written in the timeline that Bone and Loraine would come to perform certain tasks, one, being to save the life of his own great grandmother, Deputy US Marshal Fiona Miller Flynn. He took a bullet meant for her and actually died for a few moments."

"You're kidding."

"No, I got there just in time and with the help of Fiona's life energy, we were able to bring him back."

"Nothing in the papers about that."

Lucy nodded. "I'm not surprised. We didn't tell anyone…And shortly after that he and Loraine were part of a group that saved the future president of the United States, Theodore Roosevelt…"

"Ah, the hunting trip to the Kiamichis."

"Yes. Both *Anompoli Lawa* and I were along."

"The newspaper article I discovered in my time didn't mention everyone that was along on the trip."

"*Anomopli Lawa* is also known as Doctor Winchester Ashalatubbi of the Chickasaw Nation.

He's a medical doctor as well as a doctor of divinity and the tribal Shaman."

"Interesting."

"Maybe you'll get to meet him while you're here. He's an amazingly brilliant man…He said…and this is so simple that it more than makes sense once you understand the space and time continuum…'If you travel to the past, then you are part of the past…and always have been.'"

"But…"

"Yes, I know. When we meet in 2014, I will already know of you because you had come back to this time, but I felt it would not be proper to tell you then…"

"Ah…Then I was right when I told Captain St. John I had already been back here. I suppose it's like the Temporal Prime Directive stating that history must not be changed or tampered with and the timeline must be protected…plus the standard Prime Directive from the TV show and movies in my time, *Star Trek*, of prohibiting interference with other world's cultures…" said Padrino. "It just wasn't the right time for us to know that we would be traveling back in time."

Lucy nodded. “So you see how *Anompoli Lawa’s* ancient Amerindian explanation fits…You have always been here.”

Padrino shook his head and blew out his breath. “It is amazingly simple and amazingly complicated at the same time.” He grinned. “The nuances of the folds in the space and time continuum.”

Lucy added, “That fictional show is very close to being right on quite a number of things.”

“It’s rumored that the show’s creator, Gene Rodenberry, got many of his ideas for the series from actually visiting with aliens.”

Her eyes twinkled. “Could be…But now, you’re mostly caught up…except for what is going to happen before you go back to your time.”

“So, we will be going back?”

“That’s the way things stand…for now.”

Padrino arched his white eyebrows.

“Welcome to our home, Padrino,” said Mary Lou as she came out the green painted gingerbread screen door. She was followed by her husband, Cletus. “Lucy’s told us all about you.”

He snatched his veteran’s ball cap from his head. “Miz Wilson. I’m really happy to meet you.” He sniffed the air. “Well, that smells very good.”

"Since Lucy told us you were comin', I waited supper till you got here. I fried up a couple of pullets, with smashed potatoes, cream gravy, put by field peas and fresh yeast rolls."

Padrino grinned. "Nothing can beat fresh yeast rolls and butter."

Mary Lou grinned. "Unless it's my pickled peach cobbler."

Lucy could almost see Padrino's mouth watering and grinned.

"Oh, my," he said.

"Cletus, why don't you take care of Padrino's mounts."

"I'll help, Miz Wilson."

"Oh, nonsense, you're a guest and have had a hard ride to get here…Now you come on inside, I'll pour you up a mug of cold sweet tea…The ice man came today."

"It's no problem, Padrino," said Cletus. "I'm still confused how that mind conversation thing ya'll do works, though."

Lucy looked at her adoptive father. "It's not really a conversation, Papa. People don't think in words…We actually just exchange impressions and images. The thought process, in other words."

He shook his head as he walked down toward the horses and muttered, “Still don’t get it.”

JACKSBORO, TEXAS

The door to the Sheriff's office opened and Gomer’s intended, Emma Lou, came in carrying his supper on a wooden tray.

“Come on in girly,” said Harlan Rudabaugh.

She looked at the two hardcases with more than a little trepidation. “Who are you and where’s Gomer?”

“He’s back in a cell. Now set that grub on the desk here an’ you go back and bring some more fer me an’ my brother here,” added Frank.

“But what about Gomer?” she asked.

The two brothers exchanged glances.

“He’ll be fine, long as you do what yer tol’…*Sabe*?…Now bring two suppers an’ tell yer boss that she’s to feed our men whenever they come in.…What’s the name of yer eatin’ place?”

“Sewell’s Restaurant.”

“Awright then…Git.” Harlan pointed to the door.

One of the Rudabaugh's men, Luke Brogan, came in the door as Emma Lou was leaving. He glanced at her with an appraising eye, and then closed the door behind him.

"May have me some of that 'fore we go..." He turned to the two brothers. "Got the lookouts posted on all sides of town...We'll know if'n anybody's comin'."

"Who'd you put out there?" asked Frank.

"Apache Kid on the east, Boone on the west, Doc on the north, an' Joshua, the south, fer the first shift."

"Good choices. They know not to kill anybody till we find out who they are, right?" inquired Harlan.

"What if'n somebody puts up a fight?"

"The boys'll already have the drop on 'em, so tell 'em to jest wing 'em," said Frank.

"An' tell the boys they kin go to that Sewell's place to eat, got it?" added Harlan.

"How long you think we'll have to wait?"

"Long as we have to," answered Frank turning back to the stove and grabbing the coffee pot with his bandana and filling one of Sheriff Flynn's white ceramic cups from the shelf above the stove.

"Tell Black Jack to come in here. He should be just outside."

Luke nodded and headed back out the door.

In a short moment, Black Jack Webb, a hawkish looking man with close set, dark eyes, stuck his head in the door. "What?"

"There's a nigger that works at a horse ranch, the Flyin' L, southeast of here. Name's Slim Parker…I want him," said Frank. "Alive."

"Got it," replied Black Jack.

§§§

CHAPTER SEVENTEEN

NORTH TEXAS

The train chugged its way out of Valley View, only ten miles from Gainesville to the north. It was almost midnight.

A troubled Bone leaned over to Loraine. "You're not going to believe this, Pard."

She stirred from her intermittent slumber in the rocking and swaying railroad car. “What’s that, hon?”

“I think Padrino’s here.”

Loraine jerked up, fully awake and turned to him. “What did you say?”

“I think my Padrino’s here…in this time frame.”

“What? How?”

“Beats hell out of me…But I feel him, plus the distinct impression of danger.”

“Where could he be?”

“The only place I can think of…the ranch.”

“The ranch?…Yours and his ranch?”

“Yep. I think he’s there…With Lucy.”

“But how could he possibly be here in this time?”

Bone glanced back down at her. “Most likely the same way we are…Remember that brief phone call I got from the Captain on our wedding day?”

“Of course.”

“Using my remarkable talents as a detective…I deduced that has something to do with Padrino being here.”

“Damn you, Bone, why can’t you be serious once in a while?”

"I am, Love. I know I feel him and that's the only thing that makes sense."

"You have a point."

"I know…I also know we need to get there ASAP. I think there's trouble in River City."

"Do what?"

"With a capital 'T'."

"Oh, *Music Man*," Loraine said.

"Good, Pard."

"Damn you, Bone, I'm going to kill you."

Fiona leaned out into the asileway from the other side. "Are ya'll romancing again?…What are you talking about?"

"Bone's sensing his Padrino…his Godfather," answered Loraine.

Fiona furrowed her brow. "I'm getting some disquieting feelings from Lucy, too."

"He's with her at the ranch," said Bone.

"How do you know?" asked Loraine.

"Lucy just told me…Well, not in so many words, but in her impression of him."

"I wish we were as good at this as she is," added Fiona.

"Practice, practice, practice," said Bone.

Mason had aroused, caught the gist of the conversation, and rubbed the sleep from his eyes. "I asked Bodie to bring our mounts up from the Sullivant ranch in the telegram and put 'em in Faye's carriage house. Told him we wouldn't stay long in Gainesville and needed to get back to Jacksboro."

He looked at his pregnant wife. "But, you, my dear, will have to come by carriage. Bodie has agreed to drive you."

"Now you listen to me, mister…I'm perfectly…"

"I know you are, honey, but you're also a little over three months along…You know what Doc Mosier said about horsebackin', or in your case, mulebackin'…I feel like we're going to be ridin' hard."

Fiona took a deep breath and looked out the window at the bright moonlit night. "I know…You're right."

"I'm with Mason. Whatever's going on…I suspect we need to get there quickly," commented Loraine.

"I'm glad the ranch is on the way…We can stop and see what's up with Padrino," said Bone.

"I'd say we leave about sunup," added Mason.

"Just hope we don't get a blue norther," said Loraine.

"You had to bring that up, didn't you, Pard?"

She smiled. "Call 'em like I see 'em."

WILSON RANCH

Lucy and Padrino sat in front of the fire in the parlor, finishing their evening coffee before retiring. Mary Lou and Cletus had already gone to bed, but Padrino and Lucy wanted to stay up and visit.

She smiled. "They're on their way."

"Bone and Loraine?"

"Plus Mason and Fiona. They're almost back to Gainesville on the train…Be leaving for here in the morning by horseback…except for Fiona."

"She's not coming?" asked Padrino.

"Oh, yes, but she's three months pregnant and shouldn't be riding. Bodie's bringing her by carriage. It will take them longer."

"Of course."

"Did you find out how many there were in the gang?" asked Lucy.

Padrino shook his head. “The travelers didn’t say, but if they’re holding the entire town hostage, I would surmise that there are ten or better…Guess we’ll be finding out.

“Wish you’d given me one of those bracelets like the one you gave Bone and that you wear. Might be a good idea for both he and I go behind the lines…so to speak.” He grinned. “It worked beautifully when Bone took or will take down those evil men that were going to burn you out in 2014…Scared the water out of them.”

She giggled. “Yes, I can see how that would be beneficial.”

“He materialized right in front of one of the main bad guys who said, ‘Where in the hell did you come from?’ and Bone replied, ‘Oh, I had the *Asgard* beam me down.”

“Yes, your Norse God.”

“Well, actually Bone called your race of the *Annunaki*, the *Asgard* because of the way they’re depicted on the TV show, SG-1,” said Padrino.

Lucy nodded with a twinkle in her eye. “Yes, I know.”

She unsnapped the magnetic clasp holding her bracelet of invisibility together and handed it to Padrino. "See if you can get this on."

"Your own bracelet?"

"I shouldn't be needing it anytime soon."

The wiry Padrino laid it across his wrist and bracing it against his leg, managed to close the clasp. "Tight, but, it'll work…Good thing I have small bones."

"Do you know how to use it?" she asked.

Padrino nodded. "Bone showed me on his. I assume this one works the same?"

"It does."

He held it up and pointed to two of the turquoise type gems set in the solid gold links. "These two activate the light bending field for the invisibility and these two turn it off…correct?"

"Yes…and that one there adds the solid particle force field which will stop a bullet,"

"Really?"

"Yes, but just make sure you keep the ruby charging crystal exposed to the sun's rays…to keep it powered…The force field takes more power than just the light bending function."

"Ah, in sequence, I suppose?"

"You suppose correctly…There's a third one that adds an energy beam force field…but no one on this world has that in this time period."

"I see."

"I don't have the materials or tools with me to make any more." Lucy smiled. "Mason wanted one when I demonstrated it for him…The gold and gems are easy enough to come by, but the tiny integrated circuitry chips aren't."

"They'll be invented in our time. They literally revolutionize the world, with computers, weapons, satellites and communications equipment."

"I gathered that from you and Bone's knowledge…I suspect my people will give it to you."

Padrino nodded. "In a roundabout way…There are persistent rumors of a spacecraft crashing in New Mexico in 1947 and our military recovered a lot of equipment and reverse-engineered it…They deny it, of course."

"Was it near the 34th parallel?"

"Between the 33rd and 34th."

"They were apparently trying to get to the 34th parallel. That's near a magnetic ley line that's part of the Tellus Energy Grid on your world that we use to recharge our power batteries."

"Your crash at Aurora, Texas is also between the 33rd and 34th parallel wasn't it?"

Lucy nodded and a wistful look came into her eyes followed by tears. "My mate, *Garin* and I were also trying to get to the 34th, but it's a different ley line in Texas that runs southwest to northeast and crosses the 34th parallel near Aurora. We spiraled in from outer space closer to that one...The two lines join over your city of Indianapolis, with numerous others."

"I suspect the electromagnetic vortex that sent Bone, Loraine and me here is on a ley line?"

"Yes, they go all over the world."

"I'm really sorry about *Garin, Annuna*. I know you miss your mate."

She took a breath. "Everyday, Padrino. Every single day." Lucy wiped the tears from her cheeks. "Were there any survivors in the 1947 crash?"

He nodded. "According to my information they were taken to Wright-Patterson AFB...but they really kept it close to the vest...still do, for that matter...The occupants were said to be small humanoid individuals in gray formfitting suits."

"Like mine?"

"Like yours."

§§§

CHAPTER EIGHTEEN

SANTA FE DEPOT
GAINESVILLE, 1898

Bodie was standing near the front of the first passenger car as the train slowed to a stop. It was almost onc o'clock in the morning.

Bone and Mason stepped off first and offered their hands as Fiona and Loraine exited.

"Pretty much on time, folks," said Bodie.

"Seems like the last fifty miles was the longest," commented Fiona. "Thanks for staying up and waiting for us."

"Not a problem. Ya'll would do the same for me…wouldn't you?"

Bone and Mason exchanged glances.

"We might have to think about it some," said Bone.

"But, most likely," added Mason. "Lead the way, garcon."

Bodie took Fiona and Loraine's carpet bags, turned and headed to the street, appropriately named, Depot Lane, in front of the depot. The carriage they had rented from Mom in Jacksboro was parked at the hand cut limestone curb.

"Your horses are at Faye's carriage house, like you asked," said Bodie. "What time ya'll want to leave of the mornin'?"

"'Bout sunup, I'd say," answered Mason looking at the others.

"Faye's got a little snack made up for ya'll when we get to the house."

"She didn't stay up, did she?" asked Loraine.

Bodie looked askance at her. "Now, what do you think?"

"Wish she wouldn't do that," said Fiona. "She's so sweet."

"What's the big rush?" asked Bodie.

"We've been getting impressions from Lucy that there are problems in Jacksboro…Some kind of gang," commented Fiona.

"Plus my Godfather, Padrino, from our time is somehow here and at the Wilson's. I sensed from him that there's big trouble," said Bone.

Bodie nodded. "Good thing I'm comin' along drivin' Fiona. Gonna trail Lakota Moon from the carriage."

"Got a feeling you might need to bring along extra ammo," added Bone.

"Always do, when I'm on the trail."

GAINESVILLE PD
2018

"Oh, golly, Peach, look here, look here," said Stella.

Peach Presley stepped in the door with two cups of coffee from the break room.

"My goodness, don't get so excited you pee your pants, girl." The tall brunette forensics technician set the coffee on Stella's desk and pulled a chair over so she could see the monitor.

"Guess the captain and Padrino didn't scroll down far enough to see this picture. Can you believe it?"

"Oh, honey, I can believe almost anything where Bone's involved."

Peach leaned forward after taking a sip of the two day old coffee, and then screeched, spraying coffee on the desk and the monitor.

"Now look what you've done," said Stella as she got to her feet and pulled four or five tissues from a box on Loraine's desk.

She wiped up the coffee spray, dabbing it from a supplemental arrest report that was also laying on her desk, partially filled out.

"Well, kiss a fat baby, that is so cute," Peach said as she looked at the picture in the Gainesville Daily Register archives of the Bone wedding.

"Would you look at that dress Loraine is wearin'?" commented Stella, as she took a big breath.

"Oh, just give me some sugar…I may get the vapors." Peach fanned her face with her hand.

"It's absolutely gorgeous…and so is Loraine."

"She could charm the dew right off the honeysuckle in that dress...What's that dohickey in her hair?" Peach leaned close to peer at the grainy picture on the screen.

"Looks like a Spanish type hair comb with pearls."

"Goodness gracious...Would love me some of that."

Stella giggled. "Would you look at that silly expression on Bone's face?"

"Bless his heart, he looks like he got the last drumstick."

"Who would've ever thought we'd see Bone in a monkey suit and at his own wedding, to boot."

"Wonder who held the gun on who?" said Peach.

"I betcha she held the gun on him while he proposed and he held it on her while she said yes."

"That just beats all I've ever seen. They sure didn't fiddlefart around. Hadn't been gone less than a month."

"Ya think?" Stella took of sip a of her cold coffee, made a face and got to her feet. "Want a coke?"

"What kind?"

"Dr Pepper."

"I might could."

Peach printed out the wedding picture plus the one beneath after her best friend left. She got out Stella's magnifying glass and scanned the people in the photos.

"Oh, my…"

"What?" asked Stella as she came back in the room with the Dr Peppers.

"I want you to look smack dab in the middle of the first row."

Stella took the glass and peered closely. "Oh, my Lord in Heaven…that's a young Lucy."

"Uh-huh. First thought it was a child…Could knock me over with a feather."

"Would you look at some of these names," said Stella.

"My goodness…The captain will want to see this," commented Peach.

"You carry the cokes, I'll bring the pictures and magnifyin' glass."

They headed down the hall to the Captain's office and barged right in.

"Don't ya'll believe in knockin'?" He looked up from a stack of papers on his desk.

Neither Stella nor Peach said a word, just laid the pictures on top of his stack of papers along with the dome magnifier and sat down in the chairs in front of his desk.

St. John looked up disapprovingly over the top of his reading glasses.

Stella and Peach both just pointed at the pictures.

He laid his reading glasses down, picked up the magnifier and scanned the first picture.

St. John got a grin on his face big as all outdoors. "I'll be damned. Would you look at that."

"Look at the second picture and read the names," said Stella.

He started to read the names from left to right, "Loraine Bone, Lucy Wilson, Mary Lou Flynn Wilson…" He went back. "Lucy Wilson!" St. John looked up at Stella and Peach, both grinning like Cheshire cats and nodding.

He held the magnifying glass directly over the small person. "This is our Lucy, about a year and a half after her spacecraft crashed."

"Close enough," said Stella.

"Huh…I'll be damned." He continued to read and his eyes got big. "Texas Ranger Bodie

Hickman...Deputy US Marshal Jack McGann, Deputy US Marshal Selden Lindsey...Deputy US Marshal Loss Hart..."

St. John looked up again. "They killed Bill Dalton in a shoot out...Wow!...Cooke County Sheriff Walt Durbin...a former Texas Ranger."

He grinned and shook his head. "Deputy Gomer Platt, Dr. Winchester Ashalatubbi...Bone and my God...The one and only Deputy US Marshal Bass Reeves."

The Captain paused, shook his head again and looked at the girls. "You know, there was one female Deputy US Marshal to work the Nations in the 1890s under Judge Parker...Her name was Fiona Mae Miller, she married Sheriff Mason Flynn of Jack County in early 1898...That's who's next, beside Bass Reeves, along with her husband."

"Deputy US Marshall Fiona Miller...'A dashing brunette of charming manners...expert shot, a superb horsewoman and brave to the verge of recklessness'...that's what one of the newspapers of the day said about her," commented Stella. "Some called her a female Bass Reeves...but most just called her Lady Law."

"Now there would be a hand to draw to…Son of a gun!…Probably the best group of law officers in the West."

"Too bad Wyatt Earp couldn't be in the shot," said Peach.

St. John grunted and then chuckled. "He couldn't hold Bass Reeves horse, or Fiona Miller's…for that matter…Bass served over 3,000 felony warrants in his 32 year career and many said Fiona was his equal…They worked together more than once."

Stella grinned. "I have the front cover to Ken Farmer's novel, *Lady Law,* about her turned into a poster in my bedroom…She's my idol. I've read everything there is about her."

St. John smiled big. "Well, grab hold of your butts, ladies…And would you believe that she and Sheriff Mason Flynn are Bone's great grand parents?"

"Oh, you hush up," said Peach.

"Surely you're jesting, Captain," commented Stella.

"Kid you not," responded St. John.

JACKSBORO, TEXAS
1898

The door to the sheriff's office burst open and Black Jack Webb pushed a bloodied face Slim Parker, his hands tied in front of him, inside. He was followed by seventeen year old Lisanne Gifford, the owner of the Flying L horse ranch and Buster Martin, her other hired hand. They also were bound.

"Any problems?" asked Frank.

Black Jack sneered. "Not so's you'd notice…Darkie here wanted to have a little discussion about comin' in, but, finally agreed it was the best thing." He chuckled at his own perceived humor.

"Put 'em in one of the cells back yonder," said Harlan. "We'll deal with them later when we git the sheriff…May have to use that blond-headed split tail an' the other one for barginin' chips."

§§§

CHAPTER NINETEEN

WILSON RANCH
1898

"This is interesting, Padrino," said Lucy as she examined the moldivite crystal he used to amplify and channel the energy needed to sling him into the electromagnetic vortex. "It's warm to my touch and there's a subtle vibration in it."

"I was surprised when I came out of my meditation to find the lake gone…I knew I had been transported to a different time." Padrino chuckled. "Just didn't know which one until you perceived my presence in this time frame and I still can't figure out how it happened to be the right one."

She smiled. "It woke me from a sound sleep. You're as strong a sender as Bone…possibly a little more…but I think you've had more practice." She handed the crystal back to him. "As to how Bone, Loraine and you were sent to this particular time…is something we may never really know."

"I've been practicing zen meditation for longer than Bone is old," he said as he got out of the chair in the kitchen.

They walked to the front door and outside.

He and Lucy were the only ones up at this time of the morning, but Padrino wanted to get on the road.

"Are you sure you don't want to wait on Bone and them to get here?…They just left Gainesville," said Lucy as she followed him out the front door.

"No…think I'd better go on down to Jacksboro, reconnoiter the situation, and gain as much information as possible." He winked and pointed to her bracelet on his wrist. "Need to know what we're walking, or riding, into. How many bad guys we're dealing with and so on…Kind of standard military procedure going into a conflict," replied Padrino.

"You're probably right…Too bad I wasn't able to bring any of our directed beam energy weapons from my ship when it crashed."

"Just as well, might cause a lot of questions by the townsfolk…Teddy Roosevelt said, 'Do what you can, with what you have, where…and in this case…when you are'."

"I know." She smiled. "I was there when he said it, but it's a good point." Lucy reached up and hugged Padrino's neck.

He turned, stuck his foot in the stirrup on the blue roan, mounted, and then shifted his weight to the right to recenter his saddle. Padrino had saddled his horse while Lucy cooked him some breakfast.

"Tell Bone, I'll get to them before they get to Jacksboro…There's a creek to the northeast about a mile, think it's called Hall's Branch, or is in our time…Bone will know, he and I have fished it…Meet them there."

She handed him a small washed flour sack. "Mary Lou made some traveling food, coffee and packed a small pot, for you."

He took the sack and tied it to his saddlehorn along with his canteen. "Tell her I appreciate it…"

"Be careful."

He chuckled. "You forget, I've always been here…as you…or your Shaman friend said."

He squeezed the roan up into a road trot toward the entrance and with the sun just breaking the horizon behind him, headed toward Alvord, only fifteen miles away.

COOKE COUNTY
1898

The three law officers rode with the bright early morning sun warming their backs as they left Gainesville, headed southwest past the small farming town of Era.

Bodie and Fiona, in the carriage behind them, were slowly falling back as Bodie kept the two horses pulling the carriage at a more moderate pace so it wouldn't be so rough on Fiona.

"When do you think we'll get to your sister's place, Mason?" asked Loraine.

"At this pace…I'd say 'bout five hours, give or take."

"Hey, just in time for lunch."

"Damn you, Bone, is that all you think about…eating?" snapped Loraine.

He chuckled. "Well…not quite all, hon. I'd say it's number two on the list."

"Do I need to ask what number one is…Oh, never mind, I already know." She blushed.

"Man cannot live by bread alone…He's gotta have…"

"Bone! Hush…hush, just hush."

"You brought it up, babe. Just being honest."

"Be honest some other time."

He grinned. "If you insist…my *acushla*."

"Oh, Lord," she muttered.

"You can't win, Loraine," said Mason, who had been chuckling at their exchange.

"I know…You'd think I'd learn."

JACKSBORO, TEXAS

"Luke, go down an' tell that little redhead to bring us some lunch an' a pot of fresh coffee," said Frank. "Harlan's coffee can take the rust off'n an' old horseshoe."

"Don't like it, make it yoreself," commented Harlan.

"Don't need to, that eatin' place makes damn good coffee."

"Got a point there, brother, said Harlan.

"Gonna take her a couple trips, what with all them extry mouths we got to feed back there," added Frank.

"Where do you think the sheriff and his wife will be comin' from?"

"How the hell do I know? Could be from the southeast, Waco way."

"Er east from Valley View or northeast from Gainesville, meby," suggested Harlan.

"Yeah, wherever they went, chances are fair good they went by rail," added Frank.

"Let's have Black Jack to go tell the Apache Kid, Joshua and Doc to keep a extry special eye open. They meby will git here sometime later today or in the mornin'."

"When you wanna burn that coon?"

"I'd say we wait till we got 'em all…hangin' an a burnin'…Our baby brother will be avenged. Then we kin go home," said Harlan.

JACK COUNTY
HALLS BRANCH

It was late afternoon when Padrino reined up on the east side of the creek. He found a good spot four hundred yards or so south of the road with a semi-secluded small clearing, plenty of winter grass and vetch coming up for graze.

He would be able to build a hat-sized fire for his coffee and meal a little later and be downwind of any traffic.

He staked out the roan and stripped its tack, knowing he would have to walk the last mile into town from here.

Padrino donned his moccasins because they'd be quieter than his combat boots, checked his .45, racked a shell into the chamber, left the hammer in the full cocked position, safed the weapon and holstered it behind his back, under the jacket.

He headed north along the creek, keeping in the cover of the trees and undergrowth along the banks. When he reached the road, he crossed over on the narrow, one wagon wide, wooden bridge, slipped to the side of the road into some junipers and watched the edge of town for a few moments.

"Uh-huh, no one coming or going, just like the travelers said. Chances are they got a lookout close by," he muttered.

Padrino had waited until the last minute before activating the bracelet and going on into town, knowing he only had a little over an hour of power in the small unit. He pressed the two turquoise stones—the air within two feet of him shimmered briefly, and he disappeared as the light bent around him and he started walking into town.

He passed another thick clump of cedars and caught sight of a horse tethered behind it and a dark-skinned man with long black hair with a red bandana around his head and wearing knee-high moccasins. He had an ammo bandoleer across his chest, held a Winchester loosely in his right hand and was smoking a quirley.

"Apache…Walk softly Padrino and don't make any prints," he mumbled. *Don't want to get caught like the mad scientist, Dr. Jack Griffin, did in H. G. Wells, The Invisible Man, by leaving tracks in the snow.*

The retired Marine moved out of the grass alongside the road out into the rutted, packed dirt, knowing the winter grass would show him walking and toe-heeled past the lookout. *Got one or more at each road coming into town, I'll bet.*

As he walked on into town he moved up onto the boardwalk and then down to the square. Lucy had showed him a layout of the town in his mind as they visited. He headed toward the Sheriff's office.

He moved softly and was passing the Coolwater Saloon when the tall double doors inside the batwings, slung open and two rough-looking gunhawks stepped out onto the boardwalk, almost running into him.

Padrino stepped back a few steps to listen to the two men, obviously part of the gang.

“Sure as hell wish that sheriff and his bride would show up soon. This waitin’ is gittin’ on my nerves.”

“Hell, Hoodoo, let’s go back in an’ git another shot of who-hit-John.” The man chuckled. “Free anyhoo.”

“Dammit, Nickel Jim, you know Frank’d have our hides if he catches us drunk. Probably shoot the both of us.”

“He’ll play hell…no way he kin outdraw Nickel Jim Coleman…no way, no day.”

“Don’t git yer ass in a sling…You know you’d have to fight ‘em both. Them Rudabaughs always watch each other’s back…Fight one, fight ‘em both.”

“Yeah, guess so…‘sides reckon we want to git paid, we’ll jest have to wait it out,” said Nickel Jim.

“I could eat the sideboards out of a gut wagon. Let’s go over to that Sewell‘s eatin’ house and git fed…What say?”

“Works fer me, Hoodoo…us, Luke an’ Black Jack gotta go pull our shifts, with the Injun, Doc, Rio an’ Boone, come dark thirty…Looks like Luke’s goin’ into the cafe now, too.”

The two hardcases stepped off the boardwalk and headed catty corner to Sewell‘s Restaurant across the street.

Makes eight, so far, figuring they got just the four main roads into town covered, plus the brothers…Ten.

Padrino eased on down the boardwalk to the Sheriff's office and put his ear to the door.

"Where the hell are Black Jack an' Dog," asked Harlan.

"Supposed to be walkin' their rounds," answered Frank.

"Well, hell…shoulda brung more men. Ain't sure that ten plus us is gonna be enough to cover any possible heroes in town."

Huh, two more…that's twelve, thought Padrino.

Harlan stepped to the door and jerked it open…

§§§

CHAPTER TWENTY

WILSON RANCH
1898

Bone, Loraine and Mason trotted through the entry of his sister's ranch. Fiona and Bodie were about two miles behind them.

They reined up at the front of the house and were met by Lucy and Garin who came running down the flagstone walk toward them.

"You're just in time for supper," she said.

"Really? Who knew?"

"Nice try, Bone," Lucy commented at his subterfuge. "I hope Fiona's feeling better."

A suddenly concerned Mason spoke up, "What do you mean, Lucy, what's wrong with her?" He twisted in his saddle and looked back up the road to see if they were in sight yet.

"Yes, I suppose you wouldn't know…She's been ill. They've had to stop three times for her to throw up…It's the pregnancy."

"I think I should go back and check on her," said Mason, reining Sailor around.

"It will pass, Mason. They'll be here in just a little bit…It's not something Bodie hasn't seen before with Annabel, you know," she said.

"Bless her heart, riding in a buggy can't be much help," commented Loraine as she stepped down.

"Better than mulebacking," said Mason.

Mary Lou and Cletus came out the front door. "Welcome, welcome. So happy ya'll made it," said

Mary Lou. “Now I won’t have to warm supper up…Made your favorite, Bone.”

“Hot dog, chicken ‘n dumplins. Love me some Mary Lou Wilson c ‘n ds.”

“I suppose you won’t have any room for pickled peach cobbler?”

“You mean my Padrino didn’t eat it all? He’ll kill for pickled peach cobbler.” Bone looked around. “Where is he, by the way? Inside taking a nap?”

“He left at daylight. Said he needed to reconnoiter the situation,” responded Lucy.

“That’s my Padrino. He retired from the Marine Corps as a Master Gunnery Sergeant. A veteran of several major conflicts overseas.”

“What’s a Master Gunnery Sergeant?” asked Mary Lou.

“The highest enlisted rank you can achieve in the Marine Corps…the grade-equivalent of a Sergeant Major.” Bone looked at Mason, knowing he would understand that.

He nodded. “Sergeant Majors ran the cavalry. Know what you’re talking about. Gotta be one tough SOB.”

Bone grinned. “You wouldn’t believe.” He stepped down also.

“Cletus, why don’t you take care of their horses while they come inside…Oh, look! Here come Fiona and Bodie, now.” Mary Lou pointed toward the entry just as the carriage came through.

“I’ll wait till they get here an’ do it all at once.” He looked at Mason and Bone. “If I can get a little help.”

“Sure. Just want to check on my honey,” responded Mason.

They turned as Bodie reined the team to a halt. “Whoa up there, boys, whoa up.”

The well-matched pair of sorrel Standardbreds snorted and pawed the ground, glad to be here where they knew they’d be fed and allowed to rest.

Mary Lou and Loraine both rushed up to assist Fiona down.

“I’m all right. Ya’ll quit fussin’ over me,” Fiona said as she clambered down. “But, you can get my bags, though.”

“You’re goin’ to get fussed over whether you like it or not, Missus Flynn…You’re a mite pale, if you want to know,” said Mary Lou.

"Let's get our horses tended to, give them a couple hours rest while they and we eat, and then head on to Jacksboro. It's going to be an almost full moon, so should be easy traveling. Don't like Padrino being there by himself…even if he is tough as shoe leather," said Bone.

Mason took Fiona by the arm and led her through the gate. "But not you, my love."

"I'm fine. Honest I am."

"You are now, but, don't need you havin' to throw up if we're in a contentious situation with the bad guys."

"Well, I guess you do have a point," she replied.

"You might as well come along, though, Bodie." Mason glanced at him. "You're already here."

A big grin spread across his freckled face. "Wouldn't have it any other way."

JACKSBORO
SHERIFF'S OFFICE

Padrino fell forward, hitting his head on the corner of the door frame and bounced back to his butt on the boardwalk.

"Just as well wait, Harlan, that gal will have our grub here in a few minutes."

"Yeah…What in hell?" He spun around drawing his Colt.

"What is it?"

"Heard somethin'. Didn't you?"

"No."

Harlan stepped out on the boardwalk and looked up and down the street. "Huh…Nothin'…Swear to God I heard two thumps." He holstered his pistol and turned around.

"Probably just a armadillo under the buildin'…bumpin' against the beams," said Frank.

Harlan closed the door and didn't hear Padrino roll over to his all fours and get shakily to his feet, rubbing the knot on his head. He shook it to clear the cobwebs as Emma Lou stepped up on the boardwalk from the street and opened the door.

She went inside with her tray of food for the Rudabaughs.

No one heard Padrino slip inside behind her and stand silently against the side wall. Newton padded over, cocked his head and sniffed.

Luckily no one paid him any attention. They were more interested in the wonderful smell coming from the tray.

"I'll be back with the rest." She turned and headed back out the still open door, followed by Newton on her heels. "Come on, I've got some scraps for you back at the kitchen.

The Border Collie glanced back over his shoulder at the wall one more time and trotted after her.

Frank lifted the towel off the tray to expose the two plates and their still steaming pan fried steaks, fresh turnip greens and creamed new potatoes, with a slice of buttermilk pie for desert on the side.

"Umm, umm. Dang this looks good."

"Gotta agree with you there, brother."

Even Padrino's mouth watered at the smells. But he moved silently toward the door to the cells in the back and tried to look through the four by four inch hole at eye level to the inside. He could only see two cells on one side.

A young deputy was in the first with a tall rangy teenager and a skinny, older black man in the second.

"You know, we ought to put Dog and Rio up on top of the tallest roofs on each side of the street," said Frank.

"Damn, that's two good idees you had, Harlan."

A few minutes later, the front door opened again and Emma Lou came back in with four trays, stacked one on another.

Harlan got to his feet and opened the door to the cell block for her. He swatted her butt as she passed him.

She turned and glared at the hardcase with venom in her eyes, but didn't say anything.

He followed her inside and unlocked the first cell. She handed the top tray to Gomer and kissed at him, and then gave the other to Buster.

"Thanks, honey," said Gomer.

Harlan locked it back and opened the next.

She handed the second tray to Slim Parker. "Shore thankee, Miss Emma Lou."

"You're welcome, Slim." Emma Lou turned around to the cell across the hallway as Rudabough unlocked it after locking Slim's back.

Lisanne got up from her bunk and took the last tray from her. "I really appreciate it, Emma Lou.

"Wish I could do more, Lisanne."

"Watch your mouth girlie. Jest leave the grub and git out. Need to eat mine 'fore it gits cold…Don't need a bunch of yer gabbin'," said Harlan as he locked the cell back.

Padrino had stepped just inside to see who was in the cells. He turned around and went back to the main room as Harlan and Emma Lou came out.

She went directly to the front door, but Rudabough grabbed her shapely rear before she could get there.

He laughed malevolently. "Got a nice butt, dearie."

"Keep your hands off me."

"Haw, I'll make you like it 'fore I'm through. You wait an' see."

Rudabaugh grabbed her shoulders and tried to kiss her, but she turned her head away. He laughed again as she opened the front door and turned back to his plate on the desk, but fell forward catching himself with his hand in his plate.

"Damn you bitch, you pushed me."

"I did not. I am way over here by the door…You just tripped on your own clumsy feet."

He growled. "Don't know how you done it, you little whore, but I felt you push me. Yer gonna pay fer that."

"You'll have to kill me first." She stepped through, leaving the door open behind her.

Padrino slipped through after her with a silent chuckle. He stopped. Thought for a second and went back inside.

With his .45 in his hand, he eased up behind the two men shoveling their food in. He first slapped Frank behind his head with the two point 4 pound semiautomatic, knocking his face down into his plate. Then he quickly whipped the pistol to the side, catching Harlan on top of his ear, splitting it and sending him to the floor, out cold.

"I hate rude men."

He touched the stones on his bracelet, killing the light bending feature, reached over, got the keys off the peg behind the sheriff's desk and headed toward the cells. Going through the door he stepped over to the steel doors and unlocked each one.

"How'd you get in here, mister?" asked Gomer.

"Magic," replied Padrino.

"Huh, you sound like Bone."

He grinned. "You don't say?...Well, we could stay here all day and chitchat, but I think it would be prudent to *di di mau* out of here."

"What's *di di mau*, mister?" asked Lisanne.

"Vietnamese for 'let's hurry'...That door lead to an alley, Deputy?"

"Yes, sir," replied Gomer.

"Know anyplace ya'll can hide till tomorrow?"

"Yeah, up in Mom Tucker's loft. She has the livery just next door," he replied.

"Good...Grab what's left of your food, get your guns out of the lock up, and scat...The Rudabaugh boys won't be out that long, don't think."

"What'd you do to 'em," asked Slim as he retrieved his Sharps rifle and Remington, along with Gomer's Colt and gunbelt from the cabinet.

"Gave them a little something of what they gave you, come on."

"He, he, he, that just tickles me plumb to death."

"Say, who are you?" asked Lisanne.

"Bone's Godfather...go, go."

"You comin'?" asked Gomer.

"Got other things to do before Bone and the Sheriff get here, son."

"That gang is settin' a trap for 'em," said Platt.

Padrino grinned. “I know…Gate swings both ways.”

He closed the door behind them, went back and peeked into the front office. The brothers were still napping.

Padrino stepped inside and over to the desk, he first pulled Harlan’s pistol, took out his K-Bar, cocked the Colt, and then knocked the firing pin out with the back edge of his blade and replaced it in the holster. Then he did the same to Frank’s.

“Surprise, boys.” He chuckled, glanced at the clock on the far wall, keyed his bracelet, disappeared again and headed to the door just as Frank was the first to begin to regain consciousness.

“Think I’d better hurry, time’s about up,” he mumbled.

Luke was coming down the boardwalk from Sewell‘s and passed right by a still Padrino who stuck his foot out, tripping the outlaw, making him fall on his face.

“Oops,” he said.

Luke rolled over and looked around for the voice. He saw nothing…

§§§

CHAPTER TWENTY-ONE

JACKSBORO

Padrino walked past the last town building and northeast on the Alvord road, back the way he had come in.

As he approached the Apache's hiding spot on the north side of the road, he noticed the air around him starting to flutter. *Oh, damn.*

He ducked inside another of the numerous copses of cedar that dotted the countryside, next to the road, just as the air shimmered and the power unit of the bracelet expired.

The sun had not quite set, he made sure his sleeve was pulled up to his elbow, allowing the solar and cosmic ray collecting ruby-like gem in the center of the bracelet to get maximum exposure. The only difference was the manufactured collecting gem's crystals are aligned in a single direction…natural crystals are random.

Should have asked Lucy how long it takes to recharge after completely draining it. Time to be a Marine.

He cut one of the low-growing bushes that grew among the prairie grasses off at the ground with his K-Bar, and watching the Apache, he waited until he looked in the direction of the creek and belly crawled toward another grove of cedars further back from the road—and then paused when he looked back to town in Padrino's general direction.

Crawl, pause—all the time keeping the cut brush between him and the Indian—crawl, pause. He chuckled quietly. *The Marines got this trick from them…thank you. Used it in 'Nam' a lot when I was sniping.*

It took him well past sunset to get several hundred yards behind the Apache where he felt it was safe to rise up to a crouch and run from copse to copse of the evergreen trees. In this manner, he was able to circle around the Indian, and then head toward his camp.

Once at the creek, he turned back to the south inside the tree line and to the road. He crossed over the wooden bridge which was well out of sight of the Apache's post.

It didn't take Padrino long to cover the four hundred yards from the road to where his campsite was.

He checked on his horse and moved its picket stake to another spot with fresh graze, then walked back the ten yards to the camp. Finding a spot with a couple of large rocks on the north side, he knelt down and dug an eighteen inch wide hole, ten inches deep with his K-Bar, at the base of the biggest rock.

Gathering some deadfall, driftwood and blowdown, he stripped some bark from a large limb of cottonwood and peeled the xylem and phloem from the inside. He rubbed it between his palms until it was a brown powder and piled it on top of a six inch wide, thin, flat rock he had found and placed in the bottom of the pit to help hold and reflect the heat.

Five minutes later, after he had built his teepee of kindling over the punk and lit it—he had a fire. He was careful to lay only dry wood on top of the blaze to keep the smoke to a minimum. The overhanging branches of a large evergreen holly tree would disburse what smoke there was, plus the wind was still from the north and away from the road.

Padrino stepped down to the clear, rock-bottomed creek, filled his pot, went back to his fire and set it down on another of the flat rocks, now surrounding the pit. He grabbed a handful of ground coffee from the bag that Mary Lou had included in his supplies, and put it in the pot with the water.

He laid a slab of fatback on another rock and cut some thick slices and placed them in his small skillet close to thc flames. The smell of frying bacon was enough to make his mouth water.

Padrino dug a can of pork and beans from his ruck, cut the top out with the John Wayne can opener he still had from the Corps, and set it next to the fire to warm.

"Dang, that fatback looks good…Not like in our time when they pump it full of water and chemicals to cure it," he muttered.

He smelled the slab before he wrapped it back up in the oiled butcher paper and put it in his pack. "Hickory smoke cured, um-um."

He glanced to the north northwest as a small, soft flash of light in the darkening skies at the horizon, caught his eye.

"Uh-oh…Cold front."

An hour had passed, Padrino finished his supper, and was leaning back against his saddle, having another cup of coffee.

"Hope you have some more of that coffee," came a voice from the darkness.

"Do," Padrino replied without looking up. "About given ya'll up for lost."

"Had to stop several times for Loraine to drain her lilly."

"Damn you, Bone…You had to go too."

Padrino heard the smack of a hand on flesh followed by a giggle, and then saw the giant frame enter into the firelight leading his big, black, Friesian, Thoroughbred gelding, Hildebrandt.

"Figured you would come to this spot," said Bone.

"Yeah, thought you'd remember we fished it a couple years back in our time…Good fishin' hole…Don't bring those animals into camp, unless they're house broke. Take them to the south about ten more yards to that grassy patch where my roan is staked out."

"Least we don't have to haul our tack a half a mile back to camp," said Bone.

"My momma didn't raise a fool," Padrino replied with a grin.

In a couple of moments, Bone and the others stepped into camp with their gear and threw it down where they wanted their beds to be.

Padrino finally got to his feet and he and Bone hugged, then he hugged Loraine and kissed her on the cheek.

"Well, I'm really glad to see ya'll. Thought you might have gone to never-never land until St. John got through to you on your cell."

“That was the damnedest thing…There we were at our wedding reception and I get a butt call from the future…My Captain, no less.”

Padrino grinned again and turned to Mason.

“Let me introduce Sheriff Mason Flynn and Texas Ranger Bodie Hickman,” said Bone.

“Sheriff, Ranger, happy to meet ya’ll…Coffee’s hot. Fill your cups and I’ll brew up some more…Hungry?”

“We ate before we left my sister’s, thanks…So, what’s the story?” Mason asked as he filled Loraine’s cup, Bodie’s, Bone’s, and then his.

“Ya’ll find a piece of ground to park and I’ll bring you up to date,” said Padrino.

Twenty minutes later and another pot of coffee, he finished, “That’s pretty well the long and short of it…Got your deputy, the young lady and her two hired hands out of the jail. They went next door to Mom’s and are hiding out in her loft…Got the impression the gang wanted to do something bad to the black man…like burn him.”

“Slim’s actually the one that killed the youngest. Shot him at range with his Sharps…Put a hole in him you could drive a wagon through." Flynn took a sip of the dark trail brew.

"Should be safe in Mom's loft," he added as he started pacing back and forth in front of the fire. "The Rudabaugh boys and ten others…damnation. Well, least we know what we're up against."

"*Praemonitus, praemunitus*, they always say," added Padrino.

"Which means?" asked Bodie.

"The original Latin for 'forewarned is forearmed'." His eye caught another flash of light to the north northwest—closer this time.

"Think we got a front coming, better get out your slickers," Padrino said.

"Shouldn't be necessary. Ya'll get your traps and follow me with the horses…Know of a cave about a hundred yards or so from here." Mason grinned. "This is my county, after all."

"Good idea, it is December, could be a sleet or snow storm…or both," said Padrino.

"Joy," said Loraine as she picked her saddle and bedroll back up. "Lead on, sir." She looked at Mason.

Padrino kicked dirt on his hat-sized fire, slipped the ruck over his shoulders and grabbed his gear.

The other four followed Mason through the moonlit darkness, picked up the horses and took them down to the branch to let them drink. They also filled their canteens, as the night sounds of frogs, crickets, night birds, and owls cranked up, and then headed to the cave.

The limestone cave was just big enough to house the stock in the back and allow for a small fire in the front with their bedrolls. The opening faced east, so that would preclude the wind from blowing whatever was in the front, coming from the northwest, inside.

They ground-tied their horses and spread their bedrolls about. Bone and Loraine put theirs close together.

"I'll get us a little fire goin', may need some hot coffee in a bit…Could get right chilly, too."

"I'll help you gather some firewood, Bodie," said Mason.

Padrino, Bone and Loraine built a firepit with rocks just inside the entrance.

"You haven't said how you got here, Padrino," commented Bone.

"Pretty much the same as ya'll, I would imagine…We figured out the location when the Palo Pinto Sheriff's Department found your Thing…I saw the portal symbol petroglyph on the side wall.

"So, when the moon was full two days ago…and it was a Super Blood Wolf moon, at that…I took that *moldivite* crystal I showed the two of you one time that I had gotten from a Navajo Shaman, went into a zen trance inside that cave when the moon came up, and then when I came out…I was here."

He chuckled. "Then Lucy reached out when she felt me…Shook me to my core, I don't mind tellin' you. She already knew about me…"

"How?" interrupted Loraine.

"From Bone's memories and she knew that we become close in 2014."

"Oh, right," she said.

Mason and Bodie came back in with several armloads of deadfall and dumped it beside the rock pit they had built. The Ranger set about building the fire and in a few short minutes, they had one big enough to boil the coffee.

Bone slipped down to the creek, filled the pot and brought it back.

"Thank you, dear," said Loraine as she put the ground coffee inside and set it beside the flames.

Padrino laughed and shook his head. "Still can't get over ya'll getting married. St. John was gobsmacked…"

"What?" asked Flynn.

"Flabbergasted…Stella said she knew ya'll were in love, but that you didn't know it or were fightin' it."

Bone kissed Loraine on the cheek and wrapped his arm around her shoulder. "She was right…Hit us like a freight train…guess it triggered when Loraine was shot while we were breaking up a stagecoach robbery."

Then he laughed. "We couldn't believe it either…Say, what about Tyrin?"

"St. John said he would get Stella and Peach to go out to the ranch."

"Oh, good. Got to worrying about that," said Bone.

"Who's Tyrin?" asked Mason.

"Blond and white pit bull almost exactly like Garin…she adopted back in 2012 or up in 2012…depends on how you look at it," said Bone.

"I have to say, this is fascinating," said Padrino.

“What’s that?” asked Bodie.

“Being back in time…especially to a time I’ve always loved. The water’s clear, air’s clean, no T.V. with their biased news programs and gossip, no Internet, fewer politicians, no one knows what the hell political correctness is…I feel more alive here.” Padrino looked at the others. “I like it.”

Bone and Loraine exchanged glances and embraced.

“So do we,” she said.

“What’s political correctness?” asked Bodie.

The three replied simultaneously, “You don’t want to know.”

§§§

CHAPTER TWENTY-TWO

JACKSBORO

The Rudabaugh brothers walked out of Doctor Mosier's office. Harlan had a white bandage around his head, covering his split right ear.

"That old quack wadn't none too gentle…'specially when he wuz sewin' my ear up," said Harlan.

"Mebe he wuz pissed 'bout havin' to git outta bed to doctor us…Coulda left it split like we do when we're markin' cattle an' hogs," commented Frank. "Be like Chisum's jinglebob earmark."

"I'll give you another knot on yer head, brother, you keep that up."

"No, thankee, this one's big as a turkey egg."

"Gotta find that smoke an' those kids what whoever it was let out."

"I jest cain't figur out who the hell it was that hit us on the head without us seein' 'em comin'…Hit too hard to be a ghost."

"Couldn't a been that split tail, we both seen her leave," said Harlan.

"I know…Swear to God there weren't nobody in the room when we's eatin' when the lights went out. Didn't see nothin'…Don't 'member nothin'."

Frank looked to the north northwest at the lightning that was dancing across the horizon like St. Elmo's Fire on cattle horns. "Got a winter storm comin'."

Harlan looked off too. "Good, that oughta keep the town busybodies indoors…'Specially we git sleet, snow er mebe even black ice. Don't think the sheriff an' his wife er comin' till tomorra anyways, now…We'll be ready fer 'em."

"Don't think we'll be needin' anybody up on the roofs, then. We'll jest have us an' the boys on both sides of the street…We kin pin 'em down."

HALL'S BRANCH CAVE

Everyone sat around the cave, nursing on Loraine's good hot coffee as the temperature had been steadily dropping for the last hour. They could see the increasing lightning show reflecting off the tree tops outside the front of the entrance. The distant thunder rolling across the dark skies resembled that of a battlefield artillery bombardment.

"What do we do if it's an ice storm?" asked Loraine.

"That'll be a good thing, babe. Means they won't be able to set an outside ambush for the sheriff…They'll be inside out of the weather." He grinned. "Just be sure you don't slip and fall down."

"Easy for you to say," Loraine muttered.

"That's right, Bone. One thing I've noticed about evildoers in my years of law enforcement is they aren't too prone to expose themselves to any hardships…Especially when it's related to harsh weather," said Mason.

"If it's snow, we'll have a problem with Bone and me using Lucy's bracelets."

"How so, Padrino?" asked Bodie.

"Our bodies might be invisible, but we would leave tracks in the snow, maybe less in sleet…Now if it's ice, that's another thing all together."

"Other than bustin' our butts if we were to fall…won't be leaving tracks," added Bone.

"What's the plan, then?" asked Bodie.

"I recommend we do an OK Corral," said Padrino.

"What do you mean?" inquired a confused Flynn.

"Well, according to newspaper reports, the three Earp brothers, Wyatt, Virgil and Morgan, along with Wyatt's friend, Doc Holliday, braced the gang known as the Cowboys in the street in an alley beside a stable with the name, O.K. in Tombstone, Arizona Territory, in 1881…It lasted about thirty seconds."

"Head on?" asked Mason.

"Head on...There were six of the Cowboys, Billy Claiborne, Ike and Billy Clanton, Tom and Frank McLaury and Wes Fuller..."

Bodie interrupted Padrino. "But, you said they was twelve of these yahoos."

"No matter," said Bone. "One, they won't be expecting there to be five of us and they have no idea of our firepower."

"Exactly," commented Loraine. "Padrino and I will be using our semiautomatic .45s, Bone, his hand cannon...I've seen just the sound of that thing firing make bad guys pee their pants."

"And then there's Mason and Bodie. I understand ya'll aren't too shoddy either," commented Bone.

"Right, I've got eight rounds in my pistol with two backup magazines. I can fire all eight and reload in less than a total of four seconds," said Loraine.

"That's a fact, seen her do it," commented Mason.

"How many extra mags do you have, Padrino?"

"Two also, but mine only hold seven rounds."

"Close enough," she replied.

"All right, now, here's what I suggest we do..."

For the next fifteen minutes, Bone laid out a fire fight plan.

Later, the five intrepid law officers were all cleaning and checking their weapons and having coffee as the storm was almost on top of them.

"Glad we got a good supply of firewood. Methinks we're going to need it tonight," said Loraine as she emptied and reloaded her two mags.

"Is gettin' a mite nippy," added Mason as he peered down the barrel of his Colt after running a patch through it…Sure glad we didn't let Fiona come."

"What was the matter with her?" asked Padrino.

"She's pregnant…threw up most of the way to the Wilson ranch," answered Bodie.

"Ah, of course…And you're right, Mason, she didn't need to be out in all this…She's carrying Bone's grandmother."

Mason looked over at him and nodded. "I know that 'Padrino' means Godfather, but you or Bone never said what your real name is."

Padrino grinned. "It's Jethro Barthelomew Pereira."

“I see why you prefer just Padrino,” said Bodie.

A down draft of frigid air hit the trees out in front the cave, bending their tops to the south. The wind was followed by a blast of sleet that peppered the outside with millions of tiny pellets of ice. It rattled off the cold, bare limbs like hundreds of tiny machine guns.

Bone shook his massive shoulders and threw some more wood on the fire. “Hope that slacks off some by tomorrow.” He glanced at the white wall of falling sleet outside the entrance illuminated by the flames.

“It will…I surmise that the front with its accompanying frozen moisture will be like most Texas winter storms that hit this way…short and fierce. If we were going to be beset by a long drawn out snowstorm, it would have started gently with huge snowflakes drifting slowly down…and lasting for several days with possibly up to a foot of the white stuff.”

“Hope you’re right, Padrino,” said Mason as he warmed up his coffee and squatted down close to the fire.

The sun wasn't up yet as Padrino stirred the fire to life and added some sticks. In a moment, there was a nice blaze and he had the coffee pot sitting on the flat rock next to it.

He could see stars outside. "Going to be a clear day," he mumbled.

"Don't mutter, old man, speak up," said Bone as he walked over from his bedroll and held his hands out to the fire.

"Wasn't speaking to you. Let you know when I do...Old man is it? I'll show you 'old'. You're not too big for me to still whip your young ass, you know?"

Bone held up his hands. "I give...I know you're not. They couldn't melt me and pour me on you."

Padrino handed him his empty canteen. "Why don't you go down to the creek and refill this, while you're resting...Used what I had to make our coffee. May need some more."

Bone took his canteen and headed outside and down the slope to the branch, sliding part of the way.

"Wish I could get him to do things that easy," said Loraine, rubbing the sleep from her eyes, squatting down beside the fire and filling her cup. "Smelled the coffee."

"One of the best ways to wake up that I know about…except for smellin' bacon or pancakes." He grinned.

"Heard that…Get your side of fatback out, I'll slice up some for us and put it on. Mary Lou said she put a big one in your poke."

"Mmm, sounds good," said Bodie as he slipped on his jacket. "Gotta go outside and see a man about a dog."

"That was a lot more information than we needed, Bodie," said Loraine.

Padrino got his slab out and handed the wrapped package to her. "Need my K-Bar?"

She pulled out her own knife, a ten inch Bowie of hammered and folded Damascus steel.

"Whoa, I forgot you had that. Had it on you when you transported?"

"I did…Bone made sure I had my Kimber and my knife with me when we went fishing at Possum Kingdom Lake, for snakes, you know…I came…they did too."

"It's a good thing," he answered. "We'll have to be satisfied with bacon, pan bread and beans for breakfast."

"We'll have to go to Sewell's after we take care of business…She makes flapjacks to die for," said Mason as he walked forward from back in the cave where he had bedded down.

Bone stepped back inside with Padrino's canteen. "Tell ya'll one thing, cold enough out there to freeze the…"

"Bone!" Loraine snapped.

He grinned. "Was going to say the ears off a mule."

"Uh-huh," Loraine countered.

"What time do ya'll want to head out?" asked Bodie as he came back inside.

"Soon as we're done havin' a bite," said Mason.

"Like Washington surprising the Hessians in 1776 on Christmas night," said Padrino.

"That's when he crossed the Delaware wasn't it?" commented Loraine.

"It was," answered Padrino.

"Well, here's hopin' it works as well," said Bodie.

"Paraphrasing Master Yoda…'Doing there is…Hoping there is not," commented Padrino.

"Who is that?" asked Mason.

"A character in a science fiction movie in our time about a space war saga," said Bone.

"Oh, a real fantasy type story," commented Bodie. "I read a lot."

"Wouldn't say that. You know Lucy…Her race has been fighting another alien race known as the *Reptoids* for millennia…Fact is, Loraine and I have participated in a space battle against them with a secret black ops group in our time known as the Black Eagle Force*…I piloted one of the *Anunnaki's* fighter spacecraft and Loraine was my weapons tech…We kicked ass and took names, didn't we, Pard?"

**Aurora: Invasion (Black Eagle Force # 6) 9/27/14*

"That we did, Bone…that we did."

"She learned to fire two laser cannons at the same time, in different directions."

"Really? How could you do that?" asked Mason.

"It not much different from playing the piano or guitar…You use two hands, don't you?"

Mason cocked his head and then nodded.

"You mean a battle out in space?" asked an incredulous Bodie.

Bone nodded. "Out between Mars and Jupiter. Thousands of craft. The *Reptoids* were coming to harvest Earth."

"What do you mean, 'harvest'?" asked Mason.

"They wanted to use us here on Earth as their cattle…We were their protein source."

"Aw, really?…Ya'll are funnin' us," said Bodie.

"Afraid not. I've seen them. Ugly as homemade sin," commented Padrino. "They had machines in their ships that converted us to small wafers."

"They are one reason that Lucy has to hide until she's rescued. The *Reptoids* love getting their hands on an *Anunnaki*,"

"Wow," said Bodie.

"We got our own problems to deal with, though, folks. The only thing we have goin' for us, since we're badly outnumbered, is the element of surprise and our unusual firepower," commented Mason. "Eat up and let's go."

"'I drew this gallant head of war, And cull'd these fiery spirits from the world, To outlook conquest and to win renown Even in the jaws of danger and of death.'…Shakespeare's *King John*," said Padrino as he slipped on his blanket-lined Carhartt jacket.

Mason and Bodie exchanged glances.

“Fiona,” they nodded and said simultaneously.

§§§

CHAPTER TWENTY-THREE

JACKSBORO

Frank, Harlan and their ten hired gunhawks sat in Sewell's having breakfast and morning coffee in the toasty warm restaurant. They were the only customers. None of the townsfolk were out and about and not only because of the weather.

The restaurant's front windows were frosted on the inside around the edges from the bitter cold. There was a three inch layer of sleet covered with a thin sheet of ice over everything outside.

Apache, Rio, Luke, Boone…git your asses outside an' patrol the streets. You've had enough coffee," said Harlan.

"It's freezin' out there, Boss," whined Rio.

"Did I ask what the weather was? I said to git out to your posts. You bunch of gutless wonders 're gittin' paid enough…I expect you to do yer damn jobs…or you kin hit the road right now."

The four men got to their feet with sour expressions, grabbed their heavy coats from the pegs by the door and headed out the front, ringing the two-inch brass bell attached to the header.

"Doc, Joshua, Black Jack, go find that darkie an' those kids…don't come back in till you do," added Frank.

They grumbled and followed the other four outside.

"Hoodoo, Nickel Jim, an' Dog…Ya'll git down to the jail an' wait there. Don't think the sheriff an' his woman are gonna be travelin' in this cold, but, hell, they might be tougher'n you sugar tit babies…Now, git outta here."

Outside of town, the five law officers made their way on foot along the Alvord road. Padrino held up his hand. The sun's rays made the layer of fresh sleet glisten with an almost blinding glare of billions of tiny diamonds.

"Everybody keep your hats pulled down low and your eyes squinted. Damn stuff will purtnear blind you," said Mason.

"Just around that bend up there is that copse of cedar where the Apache was staked out yesterday. Bet a dollar he's not there today, but we need to check anyway. Now, not sure if my bracelet has recharged, so, why don't you check out the other side of those cedars, Bone," said Padrino.

"I can do that."

He pressed the two stones with the otherworldly symbols inlayed in them with gold, mounted in the gold links. The air around him shimmered and the big man vanished from their sight.

Bone walked off staying in the road, leaving slight footprints in the frozen surface from his moccasins. He checked the grove of junipers thoroughly, turned and headed back to the others, killing the shield of invisibility.

"Just as we figured…Nobody's there. Suspect most of them are holed up someplace warm or are out watching close to a place they can get back in to warm up."

"I can understand that, I can't feel my feet anymore," said Bodie.

"Stomp up and down, Ranger, keep the blood circulating. The good thing is we've had to walk over a half-mile to get here. I feel pretty comfortable, but we have to keep moving," said Mason.

"Guarantee they won't be expecting us," commented Padrino.

"Don't blame them, I wouldn't either," added Loraine through her dark green muffler wrapped across the bottom of her face. "Too bad we don't have any body armor."

"Body armor?" questioned Bodie.

"In our time, we've got a special lightweight vest they developed that will stop anything but a high velocity express rifle round for soldiers and law officers…Saved a lot of lives," said Bone.

"A .45 or 9mm hurts like hell and will leave a nice bruise…but won't kill you," added Loraine.

"I can imagine," commented Mason. "But, we gotta do with what we got."

"Sounds like that Kay Star song," said Bone.

"Who?" asked Bodie.

"Never mind," answered Bone.

They entered the end of Archer Street and didn't see a soul on the streets.

"So far, so good," said Mason. "Everybody's holed up…Sewells is a good place to start."

"All right, folks, take your initial positions…Sheriff, when we're in place, it's your town, you call for the Rudabaugh's," suggested Bone. "When they start coming out of their warm places to the street…we start moving. Got it? Sound is going to really carry in this cold air with almost no wind."

They all nodded. Padrino and Loraine took the opposite flanks with their semiautomatics, Bone in the center with his hand cannon, and Mason and Bodie on either side of him. They were spread from boadwalk to boardwalk in a half-circle, Padrino and Loraine were the pincer positions.

Bone looked at the others. “The crossfire angle from Padrino and Loraine will be deadly and our fire in the middle should cut anybody down they miss…and they don’t miss, I guarantee you.”

“Have to give the bad guys a chance to surrender, though,” said Mason. “I’m the law…gotta do it.”

“I’m going to count to five…That’s all they get,” added Bone. “Bone’s law.” He nodded at Mason.

“Rudabaugh!…Harlan and Frank Rudabaugh! It’s Sheriff Flynn. Come out!…You got the guts!” He glanced at Padrino. “With your gunhawks, too!”

The door to Sewell‘s burst open, Frank and Harlan looked down the street the half block at the five.

“You’ve been waitin’ on me…Here I am!”

“Just the five of you?…Haw! You’re a dead man, Sheriff, you hear me?” shouted Frank back. “A dead man!”

“Talks cheap, Rudabaugh…but that’s all ya’ll do, ain’t it?…Girls.”

“Maybe some of your hired help have more guts than you two.” He glanced at Bone. “Meet us in the street, you got the *cojones*...You gonna hide inside all day?"

Down the street five blocks at the corner of Archer and Knox, on the other side of Belknap Street, Hoodoo, Nickel Jim, an' Dog heard the yell. They stepped out of the sheriff's office and Apache, Rio, Luke and Boone appeared out of the Coolwater Saloon two blocks closer. Doc, Joshua and Black Jack Webb came out of Barber's Mercantile.

Harlan motioned them all to come their way.

"You gonna hide behind that trash you brought with you like little ladies?...Figured you'd be gutless like your little brother was. Hidin' up in the hills and drygulchin' good citizens...All you Rudabaughs are the same...Back shooters and ambushers."

"Wow, that doesn't get them, nothing will," commented Bone. "Well said, Sheriff...well said."

Frank and Harlan had donned their coats and stepped out of Sewell's into the frigid air.

"That's got to be a shock to the system, coming from a nice warm restaurant into subfreezing weather," commented Loraine.

"Let's hope so," answered Bodie, who was next in the arc from her.

The Rudabaugh gang all had their guns in their hands as they moved to the middle of the street.

"You shoulda brought some scatterguns, Sheriff," said Harlan.

"Don't think we'll need them with your bunch…Why don't you Rudabaugh boys step out in front of your hired hands or are you afraid?" said Flynn.

"Who's yer friends?" asked Frank as he and his brother worked toward the front of their group of men.

"Oh, just three of my deputies, a Texas Ranger and a buddy," replied Mason.

"A split tail and an old man…looks like he could be yer great great grandpa. Why don't you sit this one out, *Methuselah*, hate to see an old man git hurt," said Harlan.

"Ooo, Mistake…Twice," commented Bone as he grimaced.

"We started to let that old man and the lady take care of ya'll all by their selves, but we decided we didn't want to miss out on the fun," said the Sheriff.

"Boys, I'm Deputy Bone. Now, I'm only going to say this once, then the clock starts ticking. You got till I count to five to throw those irons in the street, kneel down, and put your hands behind your head."

"Haw…"

"Two…Three…"

They started walking toward the outlaws.

"Hey, hey, what happened to one?" asked Black Jack Webb, standing next to Harlan glancing at the two brothers.

"Four…"

None of the gang moved. The Rudabaughs looked at their men and grinned as Bone's line slowly advanced toward them.

Frank spoke, "Let's do what we set out to do…"

"Five."

Rapid .45 caliber fire instantly exploded from both flanks into the group of outlaws, Bone's .50 cal roared with a deafening boom, while Flynn and Bodie's .45s snapped off round after round.

Six men were on the ground, two dead outright, one of them was Harlan Rudabaugh and four others were writhing in pain in the red-stained sleet.

The panicked gunhawks scattered like a covey of quail and were firing wildly in the general direction of the advancing line of death. The survivors slipped and slid through the sleet and ice-covered ground to whatever cover they could find at the side of the street.

Several dove behind frozen wood water troughs, two more tried to hide behind barrels of farm implements and other tools in front of Barbers, the other two jumped into the alleyways on both sides of the street.

On a prearranged cue, the law officers fired another salvo and ran to cover on each side of Archer Street. Bone, Bodie and Loraine were on the south side with Mason and Padrino on the north.

Bone ducked behind another one of the frozen water troughs, Loraine managed to find protection in the inset entry of Lollie's Millenary, Bodie laid flat on the boardwalk behind a line of canopy posts, his .45 extended out in front of him.

On the other side, Mason took cover behind the opposite water trough from Bone and Padrino knelt down inside the entry to Newly's Gun Shop.

Loraine and Padrino slammed new mags in their semiautomatics and popped off a rapid four shots each. It sounded almost like one shot.

Bone raised up and fired three rounds into the water trough that Hoodoo Brown was behind. All three of the massive 500 grain bullets with no more than a half inch between them, went completely through the trough and the gunslinger behind it like a knife through butter.

Padrino crept along the street toward the mercantile and saw the Apache Kid duck down the alley beside the store. He went into the one next to Newly's and slipped toward the rear of the building.

He flattened himself against the near wall and peered around the corner to see the Indian creeping his way. Padrino stepped out into the open alley behind the stores and confronted the Apache Kid.

"Give it up, Kid, it's all over," Padrino said.

"Waugh…Apache kill ancient one an' escape."

"Sorry to disappoint you, but that's not going to happen."

The Indian whipped out his long Green River knife, dropped into a crouch and crept toward Padrino. "We fight…Apache way."

The retired Marine holstered his .45 behind his back and drew his K-Bar, the official combat knife of the Marine Corps, grinned and shook his head. "Your mistake, Indian."

"Me no Indian, *pindah-lickyoee* dog…Me Apache…You die." He lunged toward Padrino…

Loraine, like Padrino had fired four rounds at the implement barrels in front of Barbers across the street. She fired four more at the same barrel, shredding it and many of the grubbing hoes and shovels inside it and popped another mag in the grip of her Kimber.

Dog Mulvaney, who was behind the barrel raised up and threw his pistol into the street and held his hands over his head. “I give, I give.” His face and hands were covered with imbedded wood splinters from the oak barrel and bleeding profusely.

“The hell you say, you gutless piece of…” said Frank Rudabaugh, who was behind him, hiding behind another barrel. He shot the man in the center of his back, between his shoulders, pitching him forward to drape over the shattered barrel of implements.

That was his last mistake as Sheriff Flynn put a .45 round in the middle of Frank’s forehead. He slammed back against the front window of Barber’s, crashing through it into the display of bolts of various colored material on sale.

Bodie elbow crawled toward the corner of the building where he had seen one of the gunhands duck.

Black Jack Webb stuck his head out around the corner, saw the ranger and snapped off a shot as he crawled his way.

Padrino and the Apache circled each other, knives held low. There was a grin on the Master Guns face which disturbed the Indian.

"Why *pindah-lickyoee* smile? White-eyes have nothin' to smile about when dead."

"So you say," replied Padrino as he continued to grin.

The Kid lunged again, the retired Marine flipped his K-Bar in the air, caught it with his left, like a border shift, stepped sideways, grabbed the Indian's knife arm, just above his elbow as he went past and jerked him forward.

The Apache Kid lost his balance enough for Padrino to spin around, throw his left leg over the back of the Indian, straddling him like a horse. He grabbed the front of his long black hair, pulled his head back and slit his throat with the razor-sharp K-Bar in his left hand in one smooth move.

The Kid gasped as he tried to breath, but only gurgled instead. Padrino held him to the ground between his knees with his right hand on his head until he quivered in death and was still.

He raised up and looked down at the Apache Kid. "Shouldn't play with knives…especially with an old combat Marine…You're not the first to find that out."

The bullet plowed a hole into the wood right beside Bodie, who rolled hard to his right off the boardwalk to the street and fanned three rounds at Webb's position at the corner. Two found home. Black Jack spun around and down to the frozen ground—he didn't move any more.

Suddenly the silence was deafening as the clouds of white gunsmoke from everyone's weapons except Bone, Loraine and Padrino's, slowly drifted off to the south.

Everyone got to their feet and looked around at the carnage. There were six lying in the street where they stood, surrounded by blood, one was draped over a barrel and one was behind a perforated water trough that was spraying water into the street where it instantly froze—another was lying in Barber's window.

Webb lay in the middle of the alley. Dog Mulvaney was crumpled near Frank where he had fallen after Rudabaugh shot him in the back.

"I count ten, got two missin'…"

Bone interrupted Mason. "Padrino! Where's Padrino?"

"Here, Bone," he said as he came out of the alley across the street, next to Barbers. "Had to take care of the Indian…He wanted to play with knives. Tried to tell him it was a mistake."

"That leaves one," said Mason.

Loraine walked out into the street, putting her Kimber in its holster. "I didn't see where everybody went."

Nickel Jim Coleman crept from between the buildings to the entrance behind Loraine, his .45 aimed at her back. He thumbed the hammer back.

His head burst into a huge red mist cloud like dropping a watermelon from a three story building, spraying the white sleet all around him with chunks of skull, gray brain matter and blood. He dropped to the street like so much wet laundry where he stood. The boom of a big .50 caliber long gun sounded from down the street.

Everyone looked up the street toward where the shot came from. They could see a black face in the distance, with shining white teeth, beside a cloud of gunsmoke drifting off. He was waving his hand at the group from the open loft door in the top of Mom's Livery five blocks down the street on the other side of Belknap, past the sheriff's office.

"Slim!" the Sheriff exclaimed with a big grin.

"He grabbed that big Sharps when I turned them out yesterday. Said they were going to hide up in Mom's loft," said Padrino.

Loraine turned around and looked down at what was once a desperado and shook her head.

Bone ran up. "You okay, Baby?" he asked as he took her in his arms.

She nodded. "Am now."

Faces began to appear from doorways and out upstairs windows as the citizens of Jacksboro came out to see the result of their sheriff's handiwork.

"Don't know about ya'll, but I'd like to get out of this cold and try some of Ruth Ann's pancakes," said Bone.

"The first thing you always think about is your stomach, Bone," commented Loraine looking up at her husband.

He grinned. "Uh-uh…Not the first, Pretty." Bone kissed her.

§§§

CHAPTER TWENTY-FOUR

WILSON RANCH

"They're all fine," said Lucy suddenly at the breakfast table.

"Oh, thank God…I so wanted to be there with them," added Fiona, looking up from her plate of ham and eggs.

"I'm sure you did, but with the way the weather turned off, it's doubly a good thing Mason wouldn't let you go…He loves you, you know?" commented Mary Lou.

"I know he does and I love him, but I'm still a Deputy US Marshal."

Lucy grinned. "A pregnant Deputy US Marshal."

Fiona returned her smile and nodded. "You're right, of course."

"They're dealin' with the cleanup right now after taking care of their horses…They went against twelve of the brigands."

"That's more than two to one. Oh, I needed to have been there." Fiona got to her feet and grabbed the coffee pot from the stove. "Anyone?"

"Bone laid out what he called a 'firefight plan.' Something he learned in the Marine Corps, I would surmise. It worked well and didn't last long…about three minutes altogether. They met in the street east of Sewells."

"Loraine was saved from being shot in the back by the last surviving outlaw when the Chickasaw Freedman shot him from the loft of Mom's Livery, west on Archer Street," added Lucy.

"That's Slim Parker…Mom's Livery? That's a good five hundred yards west, past the sheriff's office, from Sewells…Goodness, hell of a shot," said Fiona.

SEWELL'S RESTAURANT

"Seems to be getting a little warmer, but I'm sure the horses are enjoying being in a warm stable down at Mom's rather than that icy cave," said Bone as he opened the door for everyone to go in.

"I imagine they were ready to get out of there and where they could get somethin' to eat," commented Mason.

"Heck, it's liable to be seventy degrees by tomorrow…this is Texas, as ya'll know," said Bodie.

"Well, it's still cold as a well digger right now," commented Padrino.

"Oooh, it's nice in here," added Loraine as she removed her sheepskin jacket and hung it on a peg next to the door.

Bone handed his to her to hang also. Padrino hung his tan canvas Carhartt beside theirs.

The morning smells of bacon, ham, pancakes, cinnamon rolls and coffee permeated the restaurant.

Gomer, Emma Lou, Lisanne, Buster and Slim Parker were already ensconced at a table, eating on pancakes, ham, bacon and eggs like they hadn't eaten in twenty-four hours—they hadn't. They waved.

Molly, Ruth Ann Sewell's sister, walked up to the group. "Ya'll come on over. I've got some tables pulled together. Ruth Ann said everything is on the house."

"That's very kind of her, Molly, but does she know what she's letting herself in for with Bone?" asked Loraine.

Molly giggled. "She said it didn't matter…ya'll earned it, gettin' rid of that scourge that was holdin' the entire town hostage."

"Just doin' my job, Molly. It's what I was elected for. We don't need any special treatment," said Mason.

"Except for havin' plenty of her pancake batter made up," added Bone.

"Have no fear, she does…Now ya'll take your seats an' I'll be right back with the coffee pot."

They all sat down just as Molly returned with a gallon-sized blue-swirl graniteware pot she had to hold with two hands. Their places already had large white ceramic mugs in front of each chair.

Molly walked around the table, filling each mug almost to the top. “As you see, there is already sugar, honey and a small pitcher of milk on the table. I’ll be back to take your orders soon as I put the pot back on the stove.”

Newton padded along after Molly when she came out of the kitchen.

“Newton! Is this where you’ve been?” asked Mason as he ruffled the border collie’s ears.

“He came in with Emma Lou when she was carrying food down to the jail. Gave him some steak scraps and bones. He’s been here since…Don’t think he liked our visitors much,” said Molly before she turned and headed back to the kitchen.

“Don’t blame him,” commented Padrino. “Unsavory characters, to say the least.”

None of them wasted any time wrapping their cold hands around their warm cups and having a long sip.

In a moment, Molly came back with her notepad. “All right, let’s have it…ladies first.” She looked at Loraine.

“Bacon and pancakes, Molly. Do you warm your syrup?”

“We do, and it’s local sorghum, too…Sweet, um-mmm.” She grinned.

“Sounds good.”

“Bone?”

“How about a whole side of bacon and bring pancakes till I say calf-rope.”

“Shakespeare said it better, Bone…’Lay on, McDuff, and be damned he who first cries, 'Hold, enough!’…*Macbeth*,” said Padrino.

Bone looked up at Molly. “Did you have any trouble following what I meant?”

She shook her head and grinned as she replied, “Not at all.”

“See Padrino, I know you think you understood what I said, but what I meant was maybe not what you heard.”

“I didn’t,” said Bodie.

“See?” commented Bone.

Loraine folded her arms on the table and placed her forehead on top of them and just shook it back and forth.

"How about pancakes and bacon all the way around, Molly, we'll make it easy for you," said Mason.

"I can do that," she said. "Be right back with the first round."

"When do ya'll want to head back to the Wilson Ranch?" asked Mason. "Kinda like to see my honey."

Bone looked toward the front window. "Sleet and ice are melting, I can see water dripping off the canopy out front."

"I'm willing to guess we can leave early afternoon…Put us there before dark plus the horses will get to eat and drink their fill by the time we leave," said Padrino.

"Works for me," added Bone.

"You know what I think," added Mason. "I'm sure Gomer won't mind being acting sheriff."

Molly came back to the table from the kitchen in about ten minutes with a large tray holding three plates on it. Ruth Ann followed behind her with another tray and two more plates. One had a stack of pancakes eight inches high and almost a half-pound of bacon on the side.

They started setting the plates in front of each person.

"Who do you think gets this one?" Ruth Ann took the tall stack plate from her tray. Melting butter from a large dollop was running off the top and down the sides.

They all pointed at Bone.

"I knew that," she said with a grin and followed the plate with several metal pitchers of warm sorghum that she set in the center of the table.

"Can I have a big glass of milk, Ruth Ann?" Bone asked.

"Of course."

"Make mine buttermilk," said Bodie. "…and just keep bringin' my pancakes till I say when, too." He already had his white napkin tucked in his collar with a knife in one hand and a fork in the other.

"Say, Mason, did ya'll have a chance to look at that property that adjoined the Wilson Ranch?" asked Bone.

"Oh, the Manier place? Did, did indeed. Robert and Suellyn Manier gave us the grand tour. They're movin' to Fort Worth to live with their daughter. She just had twins and her husband had been killed at his job as a bank teller in a holdup…Nice place. Plenty water and grass. Got some fine stock on it…Noticed some artifacts from an ancient Amerindian village…Made them an offer."

"What did they say?" asked Loraine.

"Nothin' yet…Said they'd get back to us by the end of the week."

"Changes, they may be a coming," said Padrino with a twinkle in his amber gold eyes.

Molly walked up to the table. "Need a few more, Bone?"

He looked up at her. "Just a few, Molly." A grin spread across his face.

"Shakespeare said, 'Once more unto the breach, dear friends, once more'…*Henry V*…I spend half my time cooking when Bone's home," said Padrino.

"Just a growing boy…" he replied as he poured syrup over the steaming platter of pancakes Molly had just set down.

"Thought as much…Already had those ready." She looked at Bodie. "Ranger?"

He grinned too. “Just a few, an’ barely run my cup over with some hot coffee, if you please, my dear.”

“Annabel will be letting out your trousers, again, Bodie,” Loraine commented.

“I’ll just start wearin’ Bone’s old ones…” He winked at the big man.

“Touché, Ranger,” said Bone as he put a big forkful of pancakes in his mouth. “Ask me if I care.”

WILSON RANCH

“They’re coming back this afternoon…Should be here by supper time,” said Lucy as she set her cup back in its saucer.

“Oh, good. It seems like they’ve been gone forever. It’s the first time Mason and I have been apart since we got married…Can’t say that I care for it much.”

“I’m sure he’ll want to hear the Manier’s response to your offer,” commented Mary Lou.

§§§

EPILOGUE

BONE'S RANCH
COOKE COUNTY, TEXAS
2018

Stella Johnson and Peach Presley were house and dog sitting for Padrino and Bone. They had finished their breakfast and Stella was cleaning up the kitchen of the one hundred and thirty year old house.

Peach was doing additional searches on the Internet in Padrino's office for anything about Bone and Loraine or him in 1898.

"Stella, Stella, Stella," Peach screamed as she bounced up and down in her seat in front of Padrino's desk top computer with its twenty-one inch monitor.

Stella walked into the room, drying her hands on a dish towel, Tyrin was at her heels.

"Goodness, Peach, get a grip. What is it?" She sat down in the other chair beside Peach at the screen.

"Look, look!" She pointed at a newspaper article from the *Jacksboro Gazette*, December 18, 1898. The headline read:

LAW OFFICERS THWART RUDABAUGH GANG

by Clyde DeLoach

'Sheriff Mason Flynn led four others in an all-out gunfight with the notorious Rudabaugh Gang from New Mexico. Harlan and Frank Rudabaugh along with ten of their gunmen rolled into Jacksboro three days ago and took the entire town hostage, bent on ambushing Sheriff Flynn for killing their younger brother two years ago.

Sheriff Flynn, Deputy Darrell Bone, Deputy Loraine Bone, Texas Ranger Bodie Hickman and a friend of the Sheriff, Jethro Pereira, who goes by the name of Padrino, shot it out with the gang, killing them all'…

Both girls started screaming and jumping up and down.

"Jethro?" they said simultaneously. "No way!"

They screamed again and bumped fists. Tyrin cocked his head and looked first at Peach and then at Stella.

"Shut my mouth…Just like…"

Stella interrupted her. "Yeah!…That is way too cool. Who knew?"

"Is there is anything else?" asked Stella. "Keep scrolling the Jacksboro paper."

Peach scrolled slowly down the file of pages from the newspaper in 1898.

"Oh, look here, goodness gracious, this is interestin'." Peach pointed at a Personals Column.

Stella and Peach
Look behind the center receipts
drawer at the top of my roll top.

They looked at each other and ran to the other side of the room to Padrino's antique roll top desk. Stella pulled the small center drawer, underneath the roll, all the way out and Peach reached up inside the opening to the back.

"Anything?" asked Stella.

Peach pulled out a yellowed envelope with a wax seal on the flap. The front was addressed to Stella Johnson and Peach Presley in cursive.

She opened it with a carved bone with an armadillo tail handle letter opener laying on top of the desk, extracted the letter and handed it to Stella.

"You open it."

Stella gently unfolded the dry, yellowed paper to reveal a handwritten note to them both.

"Oh, my," said Stella sucking in her breath.

"Well, la dee frickin' dah…Don't this blow your dress up?" added Peach.

WILSON RANCH
1898

Bone and Loraine and the others all dismounted at the gate to the front yard of the Wilson's. Lucy had been waiting on the front stoop as she always did when someone was coming.

"You made good time," she said.

"Turned off warm and we left earlier than we originally anticipated," commented Bone.

Lucy grinned. "I know."

"So happy none of ya'll were hurt," added Mary Lou hugging her brother after Fiona had hugged him.

Bone's plan worked to perfection," said Mason.

"Providence has a way of working things out. We don't always see the rhyme or reason…Just need to accept that this is the way things were meant to be," intoned Padrino.

"You sound like *Anompoli Lawa*," said Lucy.

Padrino smiled. "Look forward to meeting him, soon."

She matched his smile. "Might be sooner than later."

"Ya'll can visit later. Take care of your horses and come inside. Supper's almost ready. Fiona and I fried up a couple of chickens and a bunch of pan steaks, your choice," commented Mary Lou.

"Maybe both?" quizzed Bone.

Loraine swatted him across his chest with the side of her arm. "Bone!"

"It's all right, Loraine, there's plenty. I've fed both he and Bodie before." Mary Lou turned and headed inside. "Need to check on the creamed new potatoes, and the pecan pie. Cletus, you can help them with their mounts."

He turned to Bone, Mason and Bodie. "The secret to a long and happy marriage, gentlemen, is two simple words."

"They would be?" asked Bone.

"Yes, dear."

"Pay attention, Bone," said Loraine.

He looked at her, cocked his head, and arched his eyebrows, and then grinned. "Yes, dear."

They turned and led their horses toward the barn behind Cletus.

Twenty minutes later, they were all sitting at the long handmade thick oak plank dining table. Cletus was at one end and Mary Lou at the other, nearest the kitchen.

Padrino said grace, "Our heavenly Father, we give thee thanks for seeing these wonderful people through the trials and tribulations of the last few days safely. We know you were watching over us. And bless the Wilson family, Cletus, Mary Lou and Lucy for their constant help. Bless this food to the nourishment of our bodies and our bodies to thy holy service…These things we ask in Jesus name…Amen."

Amen's were followed around the table.

Padrino, sitting next to Lucy, unclasped the bracelet on his wrist and handed it to her. "Came in real handy, Lucy. Right up to the point it ran out of power. Didn't know how long it would take to recharge, so had Bone use his the next day."

"Thank you, Padrino."

"No, thank you, my sky queen."

"I think we can dispense with the 'sky queen' title, Padrino, now." She grinned and pecked him on the cheek. "It actually recharges in less than an hour."

"Didn't know since the sun had already set."

"You remember me saying it charged through solar *and* cosmic rays? If the sun's not available, it's night or cloudy, the cosmic ray accumulator is working twenty-four hours a day…either or."

"Oh, right. Should have paid better attention."

"What's a cosmic ray?" asked Bodie.

"Basically, high-energy radiation from outside the solar system…the entire galaxy, if you will, and are actually more powerful than solar radiation. It takes a specially tuned collector like our synthetic ruby on our bracelets, portable power generators, and aboard our ships."

"If there were anything here that required power, we could use the generator I brought from my ship. It's about the size of a deck of your cards."

"Bone and I use it extensively on this ranch in our time. There are many pieces of equipment that require power…refrigerators, air conditioners, lights, communications and so on."

"Lucy had it all set up, including wireless energy transmission inside the house when she is rescued in 2014," added Bone.

"Well, ya'll dig in before everything gets cold."

Mary Lou had set the big platters of fried chicken and pan steaks in the center of the table with all the side dishes and a basket of hot, fragrant yeast rolls that seemed to be constantly on the move around from one to another.

After everyone had finished their meal and were working on slices of hot pecan pie—Bone and Bodie on their second—Padrino dabbed his mouth and his white mustache with his napkin and turned to Mary Lou.

"Do you have some writing materials, Mary Lou?"

"Of course, Padrino. There is a stack of stationary, along with pens and ink bottles in the roll top desk in my sewing room. There's even a candle for wax sealing the envelopes.

"Who're you writing a letter to, Padrino?" asked Bone.

He looked across the table at the big man. "Stella and Peach."

"How?" asked Loraine.

The wily old man grinned. "Lucy told me something that *Anompoli Lawa* said about time travel."

"That would be?" asked Bone.

"He said that if you travel to the past, then you are part of the past…and always have been. With that in mind, I went by the *Jacksboro Gazette* before we left town and placed a personal's ad to Stella and Peach. I recognized Mary Lou's roll top desk as the same one that sits in our office in our time…"

"Not following, Padrino," said Loraine.

"Well, Captain St. John said he was sending Stella and Peach out to house and dog sit…this house…I knew they would continue the same research I had done in finding you and Bone in this time frame on the Internet…I sent them a note to look inside behind the middle receipts drawer at the top under the roll and above the desk. I'm going in there and write them a letter right now that they will find in 2018."

"All this is givin' me a headache," said Bodie.

"Don't feel alone, Ranger," added Cletus.

"Excellent idea, Padrino," commented Lucy.

He grinned as he got to his feet. "I know."

"Now I know where Bone gets it," said Loraine.

"What are you going to tell them?" asked Bone.

Padrino looked at Fiona. "I don't suppose you've had a chance to tell Mason about the Manier place?"

"None…yet." She turned to her husband. "Robert and Suellyn Manier accepted our offer. We now own the section of land adjoining this property to the east, Mister Flynn…Merry Christmas."

"Son of a gun," he exclaimed. "We can enlarge that rock house they live in now a little while I finish out my term as sheriff of Jack County, like we talked about."

"That property is vacant in our time," said Padrino. "I wasn't aware that Mason and Fiona owned it and lived there. I'm going to tell Stella and Peach to go into the county clerks office in Gainesville, find out who owns it and to buy it in our name."

"With what?" asked Bone.

"You remember that box Lucy sent you when she is rescued in 2014?"

"The gold and diamonds!" exclaimed Lucy. "I had no need of them and bequeathed them to Bone along with this property. They're in my metal case along with my space suit, helmet, and the power generator."

"Don't forget the keys to your 1930 Cord that you keep in the barn under a plastic cover," added Bone.

She looked at him quizzically.

"You bought a brand new automobile in 1930, known as a Cord. You only drove it to town once a year to pay the property taxes. It's a classic," commented Bone.

"Oh, my, my," she replied.

"Padrino and I haven't needed any of the gold or the diamonds and put the box in the root cellar under the kitchen."

"I'm going to tell the girls how to go down there and find it and see about acquiring your property back into the family," said Padrino.

"Why?" asked Bone.

"Well, since I now know how to control the electromagnetic vortex with the *moldivite* crystal, we can go back…anytime we wish as often as we should wish."

"If we should wish," said Bone looking at Loraine. "No matter where you go…There you are."

"What?" Bodie looked very confused.

She grinned, nodded and turned to Mason and Fiona. "We've decided we kind of like it here. At least for now. It's such a unique and simpler time…Who knows what will happen, besides what's in the history books."

"History is oftentimes really almost as much a work of the imagination as is fiction and is not always what it seems…It's what whoever writes about it wants it to be," said Padrino.

BONE RANCH
2018

Stella and Peach finished reading the letter, looked at one another and ran to the kitchen followed by Tyrin. They moved the table and the throw rug underneath, and then opened the trap door down into the root and storm cellar.

They looked at each other again held hands and jumped up and down, screaming once more.

§§§§§

PREVIEW

OF

COMING ATTRACTIONS

BONE'S GOLD

CHAPTER ONE

WILSON RANCH
1898

Bone, Loraine and Padrino were sitting in slatback rockers on the wide, wraparound porch, sipping on morning coffee.

"Padrino, I get a strong sense from you that you had more reason to stay than just liking the simplicity of the time here," said Bone.

"You're getting too good at that, Bone," he replied.

"Good at what?" asked Loraine.

Padrino took a sip of the hot Arbuckles brew. "Reading other people's thoughts like Lucy."

Bone chuckled. "No, not even close. She was reading me over a hundred miles away, remember?"

"I'm just getting a feeling, is all."

"Well, it's close enough. When I figured out how I could control the electromagnetic vortex we traveled in, I figured it might be a good time to check out a legend."

"About what?" asked Bone.

"You know about our heritage from the Nazca people of Peru?"

"You've told me some about that."

"One of the things I've never bothered to tell you about was the gold treasure a sect of the Nazca took out of Peru during a disagreement with another tribal chieftain somewhere around 300 AD."

"Oh, this is getting interesting, go on," said Loraine leaning forward in her chair.

“The gold technology of the Nazca was of the cold hammered type, they hadn’t perfected smelting, so every artifact they created was almost pure gold…”

“Pure enough it was shaped into what they wanted…by hammering,” interrupted Bone.

“Correct. Almost ninety-nine percent pure…There were representations of animals, offerings to their god, even, I was told as a child, a statue of the aliens that visited them.”

“They built the lines and geoglyphs to honor them,” added Loraine.

“Yes, they built them to signal us to come back and somewhat of a homage thing that we told them wasn’t necessary,” Lucy said as she came out the screen door with her own coffee.

“You and I will have this discussion in 2014, Lucy. We discussed this and many other things for hours and hours,” commented Padrino.

“I’m sure we will, you are fascinating to visit with, much as *Anompoli Lawa*. You and he both understand the esoterical value of our visits to your early ancestors. We quit showing ourselves over a thousand of your years ago.”

Padrino grinned. "We discussed, or will discus, the pyramids in Egypt and the temples of Pumapunku. How you used your inertialess anti-gravitational technology to move those monstrous blocks of stone."

"Loraine and I will get to fly your inertialess drive spacecraft in 2014. Awesome. I think you put it that at the speeds you travel and maneuver, without inertialess drive…you would be so much Tyranian goo on the first change of direction or acceleration."

"Yes, I'm sure we will talk about that, but what's this Nazcan gold you were mentioning, Padrino?"

"My ancestors had accumulated quite a lot of pure gold artifacts that two of the sects squabbled over and one took all they could carry and went north."

"North is a long direction. Any other leads?" asked Bone.

"I'm getting there. The legend goes they traveled all the way to North America."

"Big place," said Bone.

Lucy got a wry grin on her face.

"More specifically, what is now, Texas and even more specifically…the Brazos River valley in Palo Pinto County."

"Which is underneath Possum Kingdom Lake, in our time…*Voilà*," exclaimed Bone.

§§

OTHER NOVELS FROM
TIMBER CREEK PRESS
www.timbercreekpress.net

MILITARY ACTION/TECHNO

BLACK EAGLE FORCE: Eye of the Storm (Book #1)
by Buck Stienke and Ken Farmer
BLACK EAGLE FORCE: Sacred Mountain (Book #2) by Buck Stienke and Ken Farmer
RETURN of the STARFIGHTER (Book #3)
by Buck Stienke and Ken Farmer
BLACK EAGLE FORCE: BLOOD IVORY (Book #4)
by Buck Stienke and Ken Farmer with Doran Ingrham
BLACK EAGLE FORCE: FOURTH REICH (Book #5) by Buck Stienke and Ken Farmer
AURORA: INVASION (Book #6 in the BEF) by Ken Farmer & Buck Stienke
BLACK EAGLE FORCE: ISIS (Book #7) by Buck Stienke and Ken Farmer
BLOOD BROTHERS - Doran Ingrham, Buck Stienke and Ken Farmer
DARK SECRET - Doran Ingrham
NICARAGUAN HELL - Doran Ingrham
BLACKSTAR BOMBER by T.C. Miller

BLACKSTAR BAY by T.C. Miller
BLACKSTAR MOUNTAIN by T.C. Miller

HISTORICAL FICTION WESTERN
THE NATIONS by Ken Farmer and Buck Stienke
HAUNTED FALLS by Ken Farmer and Buck Stienke
HELL HOLE by Ken Farmer
ACROSS the RED by Ken Farmer and Buck Stienke
BASS and the LADY by Ken Farmer and Buck Stienke
DEVIL'S CANYON by Buck Stienke
LADY LAW by Ken Farmer
BLUE WATER WOMAN by Ken Farmer
FLYNN by Ken Farmer
AURALI RED by Ken Farmer
COLDIRON by Ken Farmer
STEELDUST by Ken Farmer
BONE by Ken Farmer
BONE'S LAW by Ken Farmer
BONE & LORAINE by Ken Farmer

SY/FY
LEGEND of AURORA by Ken Farmer & Buck Stienke
AURORA: INVASION (Book #6 in the BEF) by Ken Farmer & Buck Stienke

HISTORICAL FICTION ROMANCE
THE TEMPLAR TRILOGY
MYSTERIOUS TEMPLAR by Adriana Girolami
THE CRIMSON AMULET by Adriana Girolami
TEMPLAR'S REDEMPTION by Adriana Girolami

Coming Soon

HISTORICAL FICTION WESTERN
NO TIME to DIE by Buck Stienke (sequel to Devil's Canyon by Buck Stienke
BONE'S GOLD by Ken Farmer
ZARKOV PARADOX by Buck Stienke

HISTORICAL FICTION ROMANCE
DAUGHTER of HADES by Adriana Girolami
ZAMINDAR and the LADY by Adriana Girolami
MILITARY ACTION/TECHNO
BLACKSTAR RANCH by T.C. Miller

SY/FY
ANTAREAN DILEMMA by T.C. Miller

Thanks for reading *BONE & LORAINE.* If you enjoyed it, I would really appreciate a review on Amazon. My Author Page is:
www.amazon.com/Ken-Farmer/e/B0057OT3YI
Email - pagact@yahoo.com

Personally autographed books available at my web site:
Web page: www.KenFarmer-Author.net

TIMBER CREEK PRESS